Julia couldn't see his _____ aviator glasses, but _____ familiar chord deep within her.

He was tall, very tall—easily six foot two—and broad shouldered. His arms were muscular and tanned. His dark hair was cut in a military style and he had a short-cropped beard.

Was she always going to be attracted to military men?

His throat was long and corded, his jaw square. *Yummy.* His nose was straight with a scar across the bridge. *Dangerous.*

What would it feel like if she ran her palms up his bearded cheeks? He had a scar on the corner of his lip. Would he be sensitive there if kissed?

He was studying her. His face was hard, set in stone.

Oh, man, am I staring at him?

Yes, Julia, you are.

"Um. You look like someone I once knew. My mistake."

His square jaw lifted. "Your *mistake*."

"Yes, sorry." She turned back around and talked to her cousins, but her thoughts were on the handsome stranger.

* * *

Forbidden Lovers is part of the Plunder Cove series from *USA TODAY* bestselling author Kimberley Troutte!

Dear Reader,

I am thrilled to introduce you to the Harper family in the first book in the Plunder Cove trilogy and (*woot!*) my Harlequin debut. I absolutely love my editor, Stacy Boyd, and my awesome Harlequin Desire team. XO. Thanks to my lovely agent, Elaine Spencer, as well.

Forbidden Lovers is about Matt Harper—a pilot starting an airline as far away from his past as he can fly. The only catch is that he must make one final trip home to where his life exploded. While there, Matt doesn't want to see Julia—his first love. Why open those wounds? But things are not as they seem and the lovers might get the chance to rekindle what was stolen from them.

In this series, characters are driven to find redemption, family and love. There will be intrigue, twists and turns. I fashioned Plunder Cove after two large Spanish land-grant ranchos in California— Hearst Castle, San Simeon, and Dos Pueblos, Goleta. If you drive up California's scenic coast, stop and visit Hearst Castle. It's amazing.

You can send me an email or sign up for my newsletter at www.kimberleytroutte.com. I adore interacting with readers.

Thank you for reading!

Kimberley Troutte

KIMBERLEY TROUTTE

FORBIDDEN LOVERS

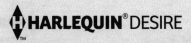

HARLEQUIN®DESIRE

Recycling programs
for this product may
not exist in your area.

ISBN-13: 978-1-335-97170-8

Forbidden Lovers

Copyright © 2018 by Kimberley Troutte

This edition published by arrangement with Harlequin Books S.A.

For questions and comments about the quality of this book, please contact us at CustomerService@Harlequin.com.

® and TM are trademarks of Harlequin Enterprises Limited or its corporate affiliates. Trademarks indicated with ® are registered in the United States Patent and Trademark Office, the Canadian Intellectual Property Office and in other countries.

Printed in U.S.A.

Kimberley Troutte is a RITA® Award–nominated, *New York Times*, *USA TODAY* and Amazon Top 100 bestselling author. She lives in Southern California with her husband, two sons, a wild cat, an old snake, a beautiful red iguana, and various creatures hubby and the boys rescue.

To learn more about her books and sign up for her newsletter, go to www.kimberleytroutte.com.

Books by Kimberley Troutte

Harlequin Desire

Plunder Cove
Forbidden Lovers

History of Plunder Cove

For centuries, the Harpers have masterminded shrewd business deals.

In the 1830s, cattle baron Jonas Harper purchased the land grant of Plunder Cove on the now affluent California coast. It's been said that the King of Spain dumped the rich land because pirates ruthlessly raided the cove. It is also said no one saw a pirate ship after Jonas bought the land for a rock-bottom price paid with Pieces of Eight.

Harpers pass this tale on to each generation to remind their heirs that there is a pirate in each of them. Every generation is expected to increase the Harper legacy, usually through great sacrifice, as with oil tycoon, RW Harper, who sent his children away ten years ago.

Now RW has asked his children to return to Plunder Cove—with conditions. He is not above bribery to get what he wants.

Harpers don't love, they pillage. But if RW's wily plans succeed, all four Harpers, including RW, might finally find love in Plunder Cove.

One

Matt Harper was this side of heaven and jetting for the sun.

Grinning, he ran his hand over her sexy, smooth curves and drove her higher. Faster. Stronger. She purred beneath him and he felt the subtle vibrations in his core. She was hot as hell, all power and finesse, sleek and intelligent. Today, he'd take her to the limits and let her break free to glory. She was made for a guy like him, not the mean old man who'd purchased her to look at her. What a waste. It broke Matt's heart to think that this sixty-five-million-dollar honey would sit around and collect dust.

His girlfriend for the day was a new Gulfstream G650ER—a sweet piece of aircraft his father had purchased for Harper Industries. Why? It wasn't as if his father was going to fly by his oil derricks to scare the workers like he used to. If gossip rags were to be believed, his father was avoiding the public and holing up in Casa Larga—the family's summer home. Matt didn't know about public avoidance, but he hadn't seen his father in ten years. Make it fifty and Matt would've been fine.

He banked left and the Harper mansion came into view. His jaw tightened. In the Air Force, Matt had a name for each sortie his team flew. Every target he dropped bombs on was called Casa Larga.

He slammed his fist into his thigh. This was jacked up. He'd rather be in battle—hell, anyplace on the planet—than here. And yet, here he was.

Why in hell had his father called him home?

He landed at Harpers' private airport and shut off the engine. Now if only he could shut down the brutal memories pummeling him from all sides.

Like his father's hands used to.

He was seventeen again, with blood in his mouth, fists up, and daring RW to slap him one more time. Dad had given him plenty of orders before, but the ultimatum that day had gutted him.

Since you won't stay away from the girl, you've got a choice. Leave now for the Air Force academy or watch what happens to your little girlfriend. I have intel, my boy, the kind that destroys an entire family. Is that what you want to happen to her?

No one could stab you in the back like a Harper.

Were the threats real? Matt hadn't known back then, still didn't know, but Julia had been his girl and he'd loved her, plain and simple. He'd had no choice but to protect her and save her family from whatever RW Harper had on them. Matt had been shipped off to the

Air Force academy that day. He hadn't gotten to kiss Julia goodbye, but he'd believed he'd come back for her. What a crock.

Ten years later he'd succeeded in putting it behind him, mostly. But what he couldn't get past, no matter how many gorgeous women later, was the girl he'd been forced to leave behind. Julia had promised to be his forever, until she married someone else three months after he'd left. He'd been cut and shot, but nothing in the Air Force hurt as bad as receiving news of Julia's wedding from home. It was the final blow and he'd sworn he'd never return to Plunder Cove.

Until RW made him a deal: fly the Gulfstream to Plunder Cove and Harper Industries would purchase the last plane required for Matt's fleet in Southeast Asia. An investor had bailed on him and Matt's new airline company needed that final aircraft. He'd had to take the deal. And, just like that, RW Harper—pirate slash oil tycoon—had bought him.

He would not hang around Plunder Cove long enough to see Julia Espinoza, or whatever her last name was now.

After this, Matt Harper was done.

Matt stopped in at Juanita's Café and Market. It was one of his favorite childhood hangouts in Pueblicito—the tiny village on the edge of his family's property.

The first summer he'd gone into the place, he was eight. He'd been overwhelmed by interesting smells and sights. He couldn't understand the Spanish signs, and the boar's head behind the meat counter had freaked him out, but the Mexican candy was intriguing. He'd never seen anything like it so he'd swiped a handful. His mother had been horrified that he'd, first, gone into that dirty place and, second, taken anything from "those people." She'd made him go back and pay for the candy.

Juanita herself had given him a stern look and told him she expected him to work for his crimes. He'd swept the entire store. It was the first time he'd worked for anything, or felt a sense of accomplishment. He'd returned the next day and asked if he could steal something else.

"Why? Didn't you learn your lesson?" she'd asked.

"Sure, I did. I want to sweep again. Work is fun."

Juanita had thrown her head back, laughed and then hugged him. She'd smelled nice and her arms had been warm and soft. He'd wished his mother would hug and smile with her whole face like Juanita did, not just with her thin lips.

"Claro, amorcito." She'd released him and handed him a broom. "Use this anytime you want. I'll pay you in *dulces*."

A bargain was struck. When his family visited for the summer, he spent a lot of his vacation helping Juanita. He had all the sweets he could want. And churros. Holy crap, he'd forgotten about the churros.

His mouth watered as he waited at a table outside for Juanita to take his order. Some of the same old codgers sat at the other tables eating *menudo* and yakking above the polka beat playing in the background. It was as if he'd never left. Except that Julia wasn't with him this time.

A young girl slapped a basket of chips on his table followed by a small bowl of salsa. "Ready to order, mister?"

"You're not Juanita."

"Good one. And you're not George Clooney. Juanita is working her other job today. I'm Ana."

Other job? Was Juanita in financial trouble? "Where? I'm an old friend in town for a few days. I'd like to see her."

"Sorry. It's a *secret* job. As in, I don't even know where she is. You want something to drink?"

Matt couldn't help feeling crushed. Juanita was the only one who'd seemed to really care about him. "Beer, please. Do you have churros today?"

"Every day. I'll be right back."

He ate his chips and dipped them into the world's hottest salsa. His ears burned from the heat and sweat rolled down his back. He'd missed this. When Ana brought his beer, she said, "Go easy, mister. That stuff's hot. I'll bring you a water, too."

He nodded and gulped beer to cool his tongue. It didn't help.

At the table next to him, two women loudly discussed dresses and shoes. "Well, I don't care if you all are going in pirate costumes. I'm wearing the new dress I ordered. It's not every day a girl gets invited to the Harper mansion."

He almost choked on his beer. The women didn't look familiar and there was no way RW Harper had invited total strangers to his house.

"Excuse me. Did you say there is a party at the Harpers'?"

The lady leaned closer. "Yes, Mr. RW Harper himself invited everyone in town."

Now he knew something was wrong. His parents had made it a policy not to fraternize with "the help" and since most of the people who worked for the Harpers lived in Pueblicito, the entire town was off-limits. Not that he'd paid any attention to that rule. "Do we know what the occasion is?"

"No, we do not, *guapo*. But if you are looking for a date…" She raised her hand.

The other woman slapped her arm with a menu. "Maria, you'd better put your hand down. Jaime is your date."

The woman pouted. "Jaime hates to dance. I can tell by looking at this guy's muscles. He knows moves that would make a girl's head spin…" She turned back to him. "You're a good dancer, right?"

He laughed. "I was taught that dancing is for girls."

"Well, that's stupid. Who do you think dances *with* the girls?"

"Most of the time we dance with each other and the guys just shuffle their feet." A voice came up behind him. "Sorry, my cousins are a little excited about the party. I don't know why. I wouldn't go to that blowhard's house if you paid me." She stepped around him and stole a chip from her cousin's basket. "Not that I'd be invited."

Julia.

An electric current shocked every cell in his body. His chest tightened. It was hard to swallow. His heart… was it still beating?

Julia's dark hair captured sunlight and reflected it like stars in a midnight sky. He knew the strands were soft and would slip through his fingers and curl around his hand. If he tugged gently, her head would tip back, revealing the long neck he used to kiss. She would squirm and try not to giggle when he nibbled and whispered against her soft skin because she was so ticklish. Damn, he used to love that.

She had tiny lines around her deep brown eyes and her sensuous lips but her expressions were exactly what he remembered. Her voice sounded like the one he still heard in his dreams. Although he'd changed in a million ways, she still seemed…perfect.

"You're not allowed to go, *chica*," Maria said.

"You shouldn't have ticked off Mr. Harper until after the big party." The other woman clicked her tongue. "Can I wear your red dress?"

Julia shrugged and sat with the women. She was taller than he remembered and those curves. Damn! Little Julia Espinoza had grown into a gorgeous woman.

"Sure, Linda. Why not? Where am I going to wear it?"

She turned her attention to Matt, tipped her head and shielded her eyes. "Do I know you?"

Julia couldn't see his eyes behind his mirrored aviation glasses, but something about him struck a familiar cord deep within her. He was tall, very tall—easily six foot two—and broad-shouldered. His arms were muscular and tanned. His dark hair was cut in a military style and he had a short-cropped beard. Was she always going to be attracted to military men?

He scooped up a chunk of salsa on his chip and promptly started coughing.

"Careful, that stuff is hot," she warned.

His throat was long and corded as he swallowed, his jaw square. *Yummy.* His nose was straight with a scar across the bridge like he'd seen a few battles of his own. *Dangerous.*

What would it feel like if she ran her palms up his bearded cheeks? Soft, prickly? He had a scar on the corner of his lip. Would he be sensitive there if kissed? He was studying her. His face was hard, set in stone like one of the Greek gods she'd read about in college. Only they didn't wear aviation glasses.

Oh, man, am I staring at him?

Yes, Julia, you are.

"Um. You look like someone I once knew. My mistake."

His square jaw lifted. "Your *mistake*."

"Yes, sorry." She turned back around and talked to her cousins, but her thoughts were on the handsome stranger. For some reason, she thought of Matt and tears pricked her eyes.

"Are you listening to me, *chica*? What shoes should I wear with your red dress?" Linda asked.

Julia held up her finger and spun around to face the stranger again. He was drinking his beer now. "Are you in one of my classes? Environmental Studies? Law 107?"

His bottle froze midair and a dark eyebrow rose above his glasses.

"Does he look like one of those pretty boys from college? No way. He's a pilot. I saw the fancy plane circling the airport," Maria said.

The man raised his beer. Didn't say a word.

"You should try my *machaca*. Especially tasty for breakfast." Linda shifted closer so the man had a better shot of her cleavage. So obvious. She'd been divorced for six months and had three kids.

Julia looked at him again. Did he work for Mr. Harper? Was he a business partner? Friend? And was he frowning? Julia couldn't tell with those darned glasses.

"Linda's burned eggs are nothing compared to my *menudo*. What do you say, *guapo*? Need a place to stay?" Maria all but purred.

He put his bottle down. "I'm not staying." His voice was deep and had an edge to it. He seemed annoyed.

"We've bothered you. Please ignore us," Julia said softly and motioned for her cousins to turn back around.

Linda ignored her. "A pilot! That's so *interesting*." The word came out sounding more like *sexy*. "Staying for the party tonight?"

"Maybe." His gaze was on Julia. Why did that make her stomach flutter?

"Oh, take Julia, then. Someone needs to get her out of the house," Maria said.

"No. I can't," Julia said.

"Got it." He motioned for the check.

Wait, did he want to take her to the party? Her? That hadn't happened in…she couldn't remember how long. "It's not you…it's…I'm not allowed to go," she said.

He sat even straighter, as if he was angry. "Your husband won't let you out of the house?"

"I'm not married. It's just…" Her cheeks flushed like they did when she was embarrassed. She blew out a breath. "RW Harper has a restraining order against me. I can't go within ten feet of Casa Larga."

He sat back in his chair and stared at her. She could see herself in his glasses and hated how small she looked. How fragile. She straightened her back.

"That's right. Our little Julia wants to sue Mr. Harper," Maria explained. "As if a lone woman could take on one of the most powerful men in America."

Linda shook her head. "Should've waited until after the party. Nothing this exciting has ever happened here."

The pilot shook his head as if he was...what? Amused? She rushed on. "Look. Someone has to stop that menace. It's bad enough that his oil derricks are out there—" She motioned toward the ocean. "We know what happens if one of them starts leaking. But now he's going to build in snowy plover habitat! He must be stopped. They're endangered."

"Come on, *chica*. You're getting worked up over little birds again. And we have company." Linda smiled at the man. "Good-looking company."

"What's Harper building?" he asked.

"She doesn't know. It's a rumor, that's all," Maria said.

"I've seen tracks by the nesting sites. A man like Harper doesn't care who he hurts." That last part came out tight, as if her throat was closing. Why all the emotions today? She grabbed Maria's beer and took a sip.

Linda chimed in. "You need proof before you can sue someone like Mr. Harper. You should've waited."

"Proof?" he asked.

"Yes. I think he's got plans inside Casa Larga. I've seen contractors go in there. Lawyers. A carpenter. If I could just see the plans, understand what he's developing—" She stopped. Why was she telling him this? What if he worked for Harper? "I'm not the kind of woman who breaks into a man's home. I swear."

"I could help you."

His voice. Something about it thrilled and teased her. Her gaze was riveted to his mouth. The scar on the bottom added an extra zing to a pair of full lips. What would it be like to kiss that scar? Or kiss any part of a man? It had been so long…

Maria elbowed her.

She blinked. "How?"

"I'll get you inside. Harper is expecting me. Come as my date tonight."

"*¡Órale, chica!* You can dress as pirates and go undercovers." By the twinkle in her eye, Linda was messing up her Spanglish on purpose. Her cousin meant sheets, not covert missions.

His lips lifted and her insides turned to mush. For just a second there he looked like…no. She couldn't think about Matt. Projecting those feelings onto a stranger would get her into trouble. Deep trouble.

"Why do you want to help me?"

"'Someone has to stop that menace.'" He repeated her words. "Like to see *you* do it."

Why? He didn't know her from anyone. It was more than likely that Harper had messed with this guy, too. Get close to a pirate and you get robbed—she'd learned that the hard way.

But Linda was right. Nothing this exciting had happened around here. The last time she'd been inside the mansion was with Matt. She'd need a strong male by her side to shield her from those painful memories. "Pick me up at Bougainvillea Lane, 3C. Need directions?"

He half snorted. "I can find it."

With only three streets, Pueblicito was probably the smallest town he'd ever seen.

"Your churros, mister." Ana, the waitress, deposited a heaping plate of the crispy, twisted doughnuts in front of him.

"Thanks." He ran a finger through the cinnamon sugar and tasted it. He groaned with contentment.

"Hot *and* sweet?" Her voice was huskier than normal. She licked her lips without meaning to.

He pinned her with his gaze. How she wished she could take off those glasses and see into his eyes.

"So, um, got to go." She stood before she embarrassed herself further. "I'll find pirate costumes for us. See you at seven."

She started walking before realizing that she didn't even know the pilot's name. Man, how hard up for a date was she?

"I'll be there, Julia," he called out.

Her footsteps stuttered at the way he said her name, but she didn't turn around. Familiar. Overpowering. Sexy. She fought the waves of desire and kept her feet moving away from the table. The pilot was not the boy she'd given her heart to, no matter how hard she wished he could be. Her one and only love had been shot down in battle ten years ago.

Matt Harper was dead.

Two

Every nerve in his body was firing, demanding him to grab that sweet ass of hers and press her up against the wall. He wanted to kiss the breath out of her lungs and never stop. Hell, he was pathetic. The woman hadn't even recognized him.

Way to crush a man's ego, sweetheart.

She walked away and he was powerless to pull his gaze off her. *Pathetic.*

"Show her a good time, *guapo*. But don't break her heart." Maria waggled her finger at him.

"Won't be here long enough for hearts to break." He swallowed the last of his beer.

Linda winked at Maria. "Good. He's exactly what she needs."

"A hot pilot to sweep her off her feet and fly away before he gets possessive?"

Linda huffed. "Maria, either dump Jaime or learn to live with him."

Maria raised her hands. "I was just saying we all could use a little no-strings fun, but Julia deserves it more. After what happened…" She looked at Matt. "Well, she's been through some stuff."

She deserved what exactly? Hell, he'd been agonizing over a chick who'd forgotten him the minute he'd left. She'd called him her *mistake*. He should charter a plane and fly out of Plunder Cove right now.

Even so, the "stuff" worried him.

I have intel, my boy, the kind that destroys an entire family. Is that what you want to happen to her?

Had his father's threat come to fruition? Was Julia in trouble?

"I'm glad you're taking her to the party. She needs a little fun in her life," said Maria.

"Should be *interesting*." He said it like Linda had. But instead of the *dirty sex* she'd implied, his word meant *closure*. If he got lucky, there'd be both.

Hell, yes, he was going to the party for answers. Why did RW want him to come back? Was it to torture him by waving a gorgeous ex-girlfriend under his nose? Was his father that twisted? If so, Matt would tell the old man off on his way out of Dodge. But not before he made sure Julia was safe.

Those were his reasons for taking her to the party tonight. It had nothing to do with how sexy she looked coming and going. Or all the hot things he wanted to do to her, with her. One no-strings night with her might be just the thing he needed, too.

He'd be her mistake one last time and then he'd leave for good.

* * *

Matt paid his bill and said goodbye to Julia's cousins. On his way to the parking lot, he placed one phone call. "Bring the Batmobile, Alfred."

There was no doubt that his father owned some uber-expensive sports car he could borrow because speed was the one thing Matt and RW agreed on.

Five minutes later he looked up when a silver Lamborghini Veneno pulled into the parking lot.

"Holy hell."

Veneno was an Italian word that translated to "poison." Lamborghini had sold only three of these bad boys for roughly 4.5 million smacks each. Barely able to believe his eyes, Matt hightailed it to the driver's side.

The window went down and a droll voice from inside said, "You rang?"

Matt leaned his head in the window. "Hey, Alfred. Good to see you."

His father's driver, whose real name was Robert, was bald now and more wrinkled than Matt remembered. "You're still calling me that? I thought you would've outgrown your Batman obsession by now." The twinkle in his eye was a dead giveaway that he was pleased Matt had used the nickname.

"Bite your tongue. No one outgrows the Dark Knight."

Matt and his little brother, Jeff, had pretended to be Batman and Robin for years. They'd christened the family driver "Alfred." Robert had acted huffy at first but quickly warmed up to the game.

Alfred got out and took Matt's pack and duffel.

When the trunk opened, the new-car smell was close to orgasmic.

"Let me drive," Matt said.

"Your father nearly killed me the last time I let you drive the Bugatti."

Matt grinned. "Nearly killed me, too, but it was worth it." Especially the joyride he'd taken with Julia. He held out his hand and wiggled his fingers. "Keys."

"Fine. But if you dent this one, I quit." He placed the key fob in Matt's hand and climbed into the passenger's side.

"Surprised you haven't quit already." Matt started the car and the engine roared to life.

"Eh, what would you Harpers do without your fantastic driver?"

Matt looked down at the odometer. "Seven miles? I wouldn't call that driving. Is the old man just petting this car?" Matt saw the flinch before Alfred righted his face to neutral. Something was on the man's mind. "What's up? Has my father really become a hermit?"

The man just sighed. "He's had a hard time, Matthew. I'm glad you kids have come home."

"Jeff and Chloe are here, too? How the hell did he get them to come back?"

"It's not for me to tell. Suffice it to say you and your siblings will hear about it tonight."

"At the party."

"Yes."

"That's not good enough. Spill. What's he up to? Does it have anything to do with Julia?"

"I can't say."

Matt narrowed his eyes. "Can't or won't? This is

me, Alfred. I won't tell my father a word you say, I promise."

Alfred's gaze focused out the windshield. His arms crossed. The man's lips were sealed, apparently.

"I have to wait to hear the big news with the whole town?" Matt grumbled.

"Yes."

Forget that, he'd question one of the staff.

"Before you try to sweet-talk the ladies in the kitchen, no one else knows what your father is planning. He is indisposed for the rest of the day. You'll simply have to wait a few hours like the rest of us."

Huh. Matt's curiosity was growing and so was his sense of danger.

Alfred pulled his safety belt tight. "Try not to run us off the road in the meantime."

"A little faith, my man. I fly jets now. I think I can handle a little car." He pressed his foot down and gravel sprayed the empty lot.

"Holy mother." Alfred crossed himself.

Matt laughed. He cut his eyes toward his passenger. "Relax. Wow, was I that bad as a teenager?"

"Terrifying." But he said it with a smile. "Always in a hurry to fly out of here."

"Yeah. I was."

"I understood you, Matthew. I was a teenager once back in the Dark Ages." He chuckled. Weird, Matt had never heard him laugh before. It must have sucked to be a driver for the Harpers all of those years. "And it seems you got exactly what you wanted, Captain Harper. You flew away."

Exactly what he wanted? Not by a long shot. "Sorry I made things tough on you."

What was his father's evil plan? Matt would find out tonight with Julia by his side. He'd shield her from any fallout and stop his old man before he could hurt anyone else.

Just like old times.

The Dark Knight drove the Italian poison straight into the villain's lair.

Julia paced her tiny bedroom. "I can't believe I agreed to do this. Why did I agree to do this?"

"Because that pilot was smoking hot!" Linda fanned herself.

Yes, yes, he was. But she still wasn't sure why he wanted to take her on a date. She was so far out of the dating scene that a guy would need binoculars to find her in the single-girl weeds.

"What am I going to wear to this thing?"

"Not your red dress. I already called dibs on that baby," Linda said. Both she and Maria were sitting on the edge of Julia's bed, painting their nails.

Julia opened the window to let the polish fumes out. "I can't believe I am doing this."

"You said that already, *mujer*. Hurry up, you don't have that much time to get ready." Maria waved her hand to dry her nails.

"What am I going to wear? Harper cannot recognize me or he'll throw me out."

"That ought to make a great impression on the pilot," Maria said.

"Ask Tía Nona. She's got all sorts of pirate costumes," Linda said.

"Because?"

Linda shrugged. "She's got a thing for pirates?"

Julia snorted. "Not hardly. She always harped on me to 'beware the pirates—especially that Matt Harper.' Super annoying. He was nothing like his pirate ancestors."

"You mean the Harpers who sailed pirate ships or the ones who bought our ancestors to work for them?" Maria asked.

"More like traded our ancestors for cattle. Cows were worth more than our people. Harpers are thieves." Linda blew on her nails.

Maria shook her head. "No, they are pirates."

Julia didn't need the history lesson. "Matt wasn't like any of them. He was…sweet."

Linda shook her head. "Nothing sweet about that boy. He used to wear black T-shirts, holey jeans and drive that motorcycle like it was on fire."

She smiled. Man, was he ever sexy on that bike. "He never crashed, not even once. And he drove carefully when I was on the back."

"He skipped classes," Maria added. "Brought you home late."

"Only a couple of times."

"Stole candy from Juanita," Linda said.

"He was eight! And he paid her for it. Geesh, I had no idea you guys hated him so much."

"I stopped caring for that boy when he broke your heart," Maria said.

"He died, Maria! Fighting for our country."

Linda shrugged again. "He didn't say goodbye."

Well. There was that.

She plopped down on the edge of the bed, between the women who'd been like sisters her whole life. In truth, they weren't even real cousins since Julia was adopted. Still, the woman who raised her as her own child was Linda and Maria's aunt, which made her their cousin. Everyone accepted her as a true relative.

Her biological mother had abandoned her, she'd never met her father and the only guy she'd really loved had flown away.

Matt had been the one person she'd trusted *not* to leave her behind. She'd given her heart and body to that boy. She'd finally told him she loved him and the next day he'd left for the Air Force academy. No letter. No call. She'd never heard from him again.

Is it me?

She took a choppy breath and her cousins both wrapped their arms around her.

"You'll mess up your nails," she said softly.

"Messes can be fixed," Maria said.

Not all of them. She closed her eyes.

She'd never hold Matt again. Kiss him. Feel his fingers running through her hair, across her skin. Listen to the heart beating so strong and sure in his chest. No more Matt and Julia against the world. He was gone, his ashes scattered at sea.

She'd suffered a brutal period of depression. Pain and loss had ripped through her with an extra pounding of betrayal. She'd imagined seeing Matt everywhere. A figure walking on the sand, a fast car speeding by, some guy going into Juanita's—they'd all been Matt. Her mind and heart had been shattered.

But she wasn't alone. Her beautiful cousins and aunts had fought to save her. Hanging on with gentle, strong arms, they'd chipped away at the black night that had swallowed her whole. They'd forced her to blink open her eyes and see the love all around her. They'd helped her pull herself together to cherish the one gift her pirate had given her—the most beautiful and sweet treasure in the world.

"Mama? Where are you?"

"In here, Henry." She gave her cousins each a smile of gratitude and rose to her feet. "Come help me find a costume."

Three

"He's here!" Henry shouted.

Oh, no. "I'm not ready! Tell him…let him…"

She was trying to pull up her fishnet stockings when her boy's voice carried down the hall. "Hi, my name's Henry. Nice to meet you. Mama says you're a pilot."

"Your *mama*?" His voice was so deep and rich that it sent shivers up her spine. In a good way. Too bad he was surprised she had a kid. Oops. Didn't she mention that?

"Help yourself to a beer in the refrigerator. Henry can show you where the costume is," she called out. "If you feel like slipping out the door, now would be a good time."

"I'll wait. You don't have to hurry," he said.

Wow. He was sticking. That was a good sign. It was

ridiculous how happy she felt about not being alone again tonight.

"Nice place you have here, Henry," he said.

Oh, now he was just being kind. Her place was tiny and old. The Harpers had built the cottages for the townspeople way back in the 1800s. The houses were lined up next to each other, so close that she knew what her cousins were watching on TV next door. Most of them were two-bedrooms with a small living room, minuscule kitchen and a covered porch. They were designed to house workers and their families. Nothing fancy, nothing beautiful. She'd spruced hers up with paint in muted sunset shades. The walls were covered with happy pictures of Henry and birds.

"So, have you flown your plane to lots of places, like, um, Mexico? Or Los Angeles?" Henry asked.

Those were the two places her son had been studying in school. Julia smiled and finished rolling up her stockings.

"The plane I flew today isn't mine. But I used to fly fighter jets in the Air Force," he said.

"Really? That's so cool. Ever been to 'Ganistan?" Henry asked.

"Afghanistan?"

"Yeah, that's it. My daddy died there."

Julia gasped and then covered her mouth. Who told Henry that? She hadn't given him many details about his dad's death because…well, she couldn't. To this day, she found it brutally difficult to talk to him about the way his father passed. She quickly pulled up the stockings.

"I'm sorry." The man sounded sincere. "I was there.

I can tell you that every single man and woman fighting in Afghanistan is a hero in my book."

"Mama says he was a great man. The only guy she
loved."

She pressed her hand to her heart. She was happy
Henry listened to her, occasionally, but this conversation had to be a tad awkward for her date.

"Give him the costume, Henry!" she called out.

"Okay. Here. Let's try this hat thingy on first. Cool!
Now the eye patch."

"How do I look?"

"Perfect! Like a real pirate." Henry sounded proud.

"Jack Sparrow? Dread Pirate Roberts?"

"Those are fake. We need a real pirate name. What'd
they call you in the Air Force?"

Julia's ears perked up. What was his real name?

"Captain."

"That's it! Aye, aye, Captain." Henry giggled.

Not helpful.

She stepped into the flowing red skirt with the im-
possibly long slit up the side—hence the reason for
stockings. The shirt was white and off the shoulder.
She bent over, adjusted her breasts and looked in the
mirror. She looked like a harlot. No, that wasn't it, she
looked like Julia Espinoza pretending to be a harlot.
Too much like herself to be truly incognito. Shaking
her head, she applied the dark red lipstick. Nope. Still
Julia. Well, there was nothing else to do but to add Tía
Nona's long, blond wig.

Did blondes have more fun? She'd find out. She was
desperate for a little fun for one night.

She came out to find a yummy pirate on her front
porch, bending over the lizard cage. She had a great

shot of his backside, which looked pretty darned good in those black slacks. He wore a cream-colored shirt and had Henry's bright yellow pirate bandana on his head. *Holy mama.*

"What do you think?" She held her breath.

He rose. His eyes—or rather eye, since one was under the patch—was blue and held her gaze with intensity. Slowly, he took her all in, starting at the lacy off-the-shoulder, bosom-lifting blouse, down her red skirt to the fishnets and red stilettos. Then all the way back up again.

The look he gave was pure heat. Goose bumps ran up her arms, shoulders, and danced in her scalp.

"I like your real hair better."

Not a blond man, huh?

"Okay. But would you recognize me in this?" she pressed.

He wasn't looking at her wig. He was gazing at her lips and she had the feeling he wanted to kiss her.

"Always."

She swallowed. She'd just met the guy and yet something inside her that had been dead for years woke up, uncoiled and pleaded for his lips.

Geesh, the harlot costume was getting to her.

He turned back to the lizard's cage and spoke to Henry. "Old Man Harper only sees what he wants to see. We'll trick him."

She stepped closer. "So…we're calling you Captain."

"Apparently."

"What does that make me? Wench? Swabbie?"

He touched her arm. All her senses focused on that warm hand on her skin. "You are my first mate."

Oh, my.

"Ready?"

No.

A hundred times yes.

Maybe.

Oh, God. Am I doing this?

She bit her lip and nodded.

She kissed Henry on the cheek and he quickly wiped the kiss away. "Mama! Not in front of people."

Just then Tía Nona hobbled her way onto the porch. "What's going on here? Another party? Oh, Julia, my skirt fits you well, but careful on the blouse. Your treasures might pop out."

"Tía Nona! We have company." Julia raised her voice for the old woman.

"I am not blind, *mija*." She stepped closer to get a better look at the man but stumbled on her last step as if her leg gave out. Captain rushed forward and caught Tía Nona before she fell.

"I've got you," he said.

"Are you okay?" Julia asked. Even in the dim porch light, her aunt was pale, shaky.

Tía Nona studied his handsome face. "You…you are…?"

He still held her. "They're calling me Captain tonight, ma'am."

Tía Nona blinked slowly and reached up to touch his bearded cheek with her arthritic fingers. Julia was mortified. What had gotten into her old aunt? The man didn't move, didn't flinch. Julia was mesmerized by the display. She had no idea what was happening. But his face was full of compassion as he held very still.

"I'm an old woman with many faults. She's my *hija*,

Captain. She's all I've got," Tía Nona said. "Understand?"

"Yes, ma'am."

"*Madre, mia*, I hope you do. One day, perhaps. For now, be careful." She released him. To Julia she said, "Never forget, *nene*." And then she hobbled into the house without another word.

Never forget, little one? What was her old aunt babbling about?

"That was weird," Henry said.

"She seems tired." Strange and old. Maybe the onset of dementia? What would Julia do without her aunt? Tía Nona had always taken care of Julia even through the loss of Matt. Tía Nona had helped put all the shattered pieces back together again. Tía Nona was the mother Julia never had.

"Be good for Tía Nona, Henry. Go to bed on time. If you need anything, call Tina next door. She's staying home with the new baby." She kissed her son one more time before he could wiggle away.

"Aye, aye, Captain." Henry saluted them both.

"Goofball."

Her date escorted her down the stairs and around the front of the house. A silver motorcycle sat in her driveway.

"Wait. That's a Harley."

"Surprise."

The emotions hit hard. She had a death grip on his arm and her teeth were clenched tightly. The last time she'd been on a motorcycle, she'd had her arms wrapped around Matt. She'd pressed into him as if he were her body armor. He'd protected her while driving them both toward freedom. When she was on the back of his bike, nothing could catch them or hurt them. Bad stuff was left in the dust. It was like flying. She'd trusted him with her life. With her love.

She'd never trust like that again.

Letting go of Captain's arm she stepped backward. "I can't go on that."

"Why? I thought you liked motorcycles."

Who told him? Linda and Maria must have given him an earful behind her back. She was lucky he'd showed up at all.

She did like motorcycles, had loved them once, but this was no ordinary bike. Oh, God. It looked just like Matt's. Pain ripped through her chest.

She turned away from the two-wheeled dagger in her heart. "I'm sorry. I can't do this. I thought I could, but obviously I'm not ready."

"Tell me what the problem is and I'll fix it."

What in the hell was going on with Julia?

First, she acted like she didn't remember him and now she was having a meltdown next to his bike? It was almost as if she had PTSD. But why?

He decided to play her game for a while, until he figured things out.

"It's personal." She sighed. "Which tells you absolutely nothing, right? Wow, what a great first mate you've chosen, Captain. Feels like this ship is sinking already. I'd understand if you want to take someone else to RW's party. You'll have more fun without me."

"I want to have fun *with* you." Like old times, only better.

"But I don't know how to…to do…this…" She motioned between them.

He liked where her mind was going. Hated the terror on her face.

"Listen, Julia. We'll dance, drink champagne, eat, laugh. It's just a party. Come with me."

She shook her head. "It's not fair to you." Her brow creased. "If you knew what was good for you, you'd hop on that Harley and go. You don't want a broken girl tonight."

He rubbed his thumb over her chin. "Broken?"

Her eyes welled.

That got him. Julia had always been fierce and brave. Had that husband of hers hurt her? If so, the dude was lucky he hadn't made it out of Afghanistan or he and Matt would be going a few rounds right now.

Hell, he was still recovering from the fact that Julia had a child with that jackass. It ripped him up. He'd never wanted kids. Why ruin a child's life like his parents did his? It never crossed his mind that Julia would marry someone else to have a child. Is that why she did? To have the baby Matt wouldn't give her?

"I can't ride that bike with you," she said.

Dammit, what happened? Julia had always loved riding on the back of his bike. His plan had been to get her to wrap her sweet arms around him and press her full breasts into his back. Then they'd cruise and he'd kiss her senseless and remind her how much she'd missed him. Afterward they'd go to the party and dance the rest of the night. With any luck, he'd wake up with her in his arms.

That was how it was supposed to go. But somehow his plan had gone south.

"Julia. Talk to me."

"The Harley reminds me of—" she blew out a long breath "—things I'm trying to forget."

That was a gut-punch he didn't see coming. At the café, she'd called him her mistake and now their adventures on the bike were things she tried to forget? Clearly, she was trying to kill their past.

"Fine," Matt growled. "You don't want to go with me. I get it."

Putting his helmet on over the pirate bandana, he swung his leg across the bike. He needed to put some distance between him and the woman who was driving him crazy. Hell, maybe he'd skip the party and leave Plunder Cove tonight. He'd done his father's bidding. He'd get the plane he needed without hearing whatever announcement his father had planned to make.

He could go back to forgetting Julia. Somehow.

"Wait!" She put her hand on his back. He felt that touch all the way to his groin. "Can you be patient with me? I haven't been on a date in a long time. I'm saying all the wrong things, but I want to be with you tonight."

"You do?"

Her gaze was on his lips. "I really, really do."

Her husky voice was his undoing. He froze. He wanted to kiss her, but she seemed fragile. He didn't want to push her—yet.

He handed her a helmet. She climbed on the bike, wrapped her arms around him and held on.

They'd make new memories on this machine tonight. Ones he could take with him when he left Plunder Cove once and for all.

Four

Matt loved driving his old, faithful Harley with Julia on the back. It felt familiar, comfortable and so damned good. Instead of winging through the curves like he used to do, he drove slowly along the coast. Sure, he was stretching out the ride, but Julia didn't seem to mind. She put her head on his back and seemed to relax.

The night was warm with the ocean fog hanging in the distance. The sliver of moon winked at him as if it knew how hard Matt's heart was beating. The breeze against his face smelled like the sea and Julia.

The long lane to Casa Larga came up too quickly. He drove under the lacy pepper trees and purple jacarandas. Luminaries lit up the driveway, making the normally private mansion seem strangely inviting. He idled in the driveway in front of a line of parked cars.

Julia's cousins were right—everyone was here. For an extra beat, he sat there memorizing the feel of Julia against him.

His Julia. One last time.

He cut the engine, swung his leg over and offered his hand to her. "Ready?"

She took his hand quickly and held on tight. "Yes?"

"I heard the question mark, sweetheart. It's going to be okay. Trust me."

She bit her lip. "I…do?"

He laughed. "Getting closer. Think the word…" Circling around, he came up behind her and whispered in her ear, *"Fun."*

He couldn't help but notice the shiver and slight roll of her shoulders. She was still ticklish. Good to know.

"Fun," she said softly.

"What we have here is a two-part mission. Part one—" he lifted his finger "—get inside the mansion to seek intel to stop plover destruction. Part two—" another finger lifted "—have the time of our lives. We're not leaving without having fun. Got it?"

She nodded.

"Good enough." He led her toward the front door.

She stopped. "Oh, no. There's a guard at the front. See him?"

"Yes, I see him. Let's go around the side," he said. He'd recognize his dad's bodyguard anywhere. The man had been one of the two goons who'd escorted Matt off the property ten years earlier. It still pissed him off. The itch to bloody the man's nose was real, but what good would that do?

She cocked her eyebrow. "You found a secret entrance since this afternoon? You've been busy."

What was he supposed to say to that? If she thought hard enough, she'd remember how to get in through the side garden. This wasn't the first time he'd snuck Julia Espinoza inside Casa Larga. He took her hand and they walked past the rose garden. Up ahead was the gazebo under the coastal oaks. He'd kissed her against the railing in the gazebo the last time they were here.

"We don't have to go in just yet."

"Okay," she croaked. Her voice gave her away. That and the way she didn't know where to put her hands. They went to her throat, by her sides, clasped.

"Don't be nervous."

"You're not?"

"A little." Hell, okay, a lot. About the party. About her. "But we've got this."

"*This* is all foreign to me. Last week I was taking my finals in Environmental Science and Law and I was restricted from entering Casa Larga. Now I'm here with a…a…date."

Could it be any harder for her to say the word? He didn't want to dwell on it so he changed the subject. "Do you like your classes?"

Her eyes lit up. "I love them. I want to be a lawyer. I really do. Those poor birds can't defend themselves against corporate monsters."

"Like RW."

Her eyes widened. "Um, and others who suck all the goodness out of the environment for their own personal gain. Meanwhile, species are going extinct and our air and water is becoming polluted. I want better for my son, for everyone."

Passion for her cause lit up her expression. God, she

was magnificent. He ran the backside of his knuckle over her cheek. "I agree."

She closed her eyes, leaning into his hand. "That's why I study so hard. Two more semesters and I can take the bar exam. Next to being Henry's mom, it's the one thing that gives me purpose. Something I can be good at."

It pleased him that she had found a noble cause. She'd always been a caring person and a spitfire. It made perfect sense that this is who she would become—a strong woman who knew her mind and fought for the innocent creatures of the world.

"I like that. Julia Espinoza, Planet Saver."

She cocked her head. "Now you're making fun of me."

"No, way. Your eyes light up when you talk about environmental law. Strong women are sexy. It's great to be doing what you were born to do."

"Yes." Her voice was very soft.

"Setting difficult goals and flat-out going for them? In the Air Force, we call that 'balls to the wall.'"

She laughed. "I don't have balls."

"Are you kidding me? A single mom raising a son while putting herself through college? Your *cajones* are humongous, lady. I'm jealous."

She blushed.

Thinking about his package, was she? He dragged his thumb across her bottom lip. Silky, warm, his. No woman he'd known had a mouth like Julia's. He bent to put his lips where they belonged.

Used to belong.

A woman screamed in the distance.

"What was that?" Julia asked.

Another woman yelled, followed by a slew of Spanish words. Julia ran toward the sounds and Matt was quickly in pursuit. They raced across the aggregate pathway and stopped in front of a large dolphin fountain where two elderly ladies had climbed in. They splashed each other like kids at a public pool.

"Tía Alana! Tía Flora! What are you doing?" Julia asked. "Get out of there before anyone sees you." Julia looked at Matt. "They've fallen off their rockers."

"Watch it or you and *guapo* will be next," Alana threatened, lifting her arm to splash them.

Flora laughed, hiking up her dress and exposing her thick legs. "Señor Harper said to enjoy ourselves. He's the boss."

"You'll have restraining orders on you, too, if you don't get out of there."

"Nope. We have to take our fun where we can get it. We don't have hot hombres," Alana said in a teasing voice.

Julia slapped her hand over her mouth in the cutest version of horror he'd ever seen. She hooked her arm in his and started pulling. "I don't want to be here when the guards show up." As they walked the lantern-lit pathway, she added, "I have a big family and they're all a little crazy." She smiled. "But I love them."

"You're lucky to have a family who cares for you."

They'd made it to the house. "You don't have a family?"

He looked at her with his uncovered eye. "I don't have anyone."

What in the hell? He hadn't meant to say that. He ignored his feelings 99 percent of the time. Julia could pull his inner thoughts out of him in a way no one could.

"Really?" The mix of compassion, sorrow and longing on her face made him want to demand answers.

I did have someone, but you gave up on us. Why'd you stop loving me?

He ground his teeth. She wasn't going to see him fall apart. They were past that now. Instead, he opened the side door and stepped into his favorite place in the mansion—the kitchen. As a kid, he'd sought solace here when his parents were fighting. The kitchen ladies had made growing up a Harper bearable.

"Evening, ladies," he called out.

Donna, his favorite chef of all time, was using a scary-looking knife to slice large barbecued tri-tips. "Busy here."

The other staff members were plating appetizers and refreshing the cheese and fruit displays.

"Just passing through." He snagged a chunk of hard cheese and two glasses of champagne. "Sustenance." Breaking off a piece of cheese, he fed it to Julia. "Need your strength to keep up with me on the dance floor."

She chewed, and swallowed a sip of champagne. "You said dancing was for women."

"That's what I was taught, but I picked up some moves."

"I'd like to see them."

"You will." He laced his fingers with her empty hand and led her down the hall toward the music. "I'm going to use them all tonight, sweetheart."

Oh, mama.

She wanted to learn a few moves from this smoking hot man. Okay, all the moves.

She'd only slept with one man—Matt Harper. And calling him a man was laughable. He'd been seventeen and she'd started to wonder if she'd ever have hot sex with a grown man. At this time in her life she didn't need a husband, or anything long-term. Where would a man squeeze in between her son, her family, school, animal activism and her budding career? No one should feel like he was the last priority on her list.

But, heaven help her, she missed passion. And being touched. Sheesh, when Captain whispered in her ear and touched her cheek, she'd all but combusted. When he'd fed her and laced his fingers with hers, she felt... cherished.

Which was a big batch of crazy *mole*. A man she'd just met couldn't adore her like Matt had.

Captain was a hot pilot who'd happened to land on her doorstep. For tonight only. He was a good choice for a few hours of passion, no doubt about it. As long as she kept her memories from jumping out right and left to attack her heart. The bike, the garden where they used to walk hand in hand, the gazebo where she'd received her first kiss... Matt was everywhere.

The first year after he'd died, she'd seen him in every guy's face, every swagger. She'd heard him calling her at night and would run outside in her pajamas to find an empty yard. It had taken a long time to get control of her desperate imagination and yet here it was bringing Matt along on the first real date she'd had in years. It wasn't fair to her date or to her.

How could she tell Captain he walked like her old boyfriend? Sort of smelled like him. And his voice, although deeper, had the same cadence. When he touched her cheek, she'd closed her eyes and Captain was Matt. Gah! She couldn't tell him *that*.

The only difference was the way he drove the motorcycle. Matt would've taken those curves faster and leaned in like he was one with the machine. This guy was far too safe on the bike for her liking.

But she *did* like him. He was sexy, strong, gentle… and did she say sexy? Plus, when he'd admitted he didn't have anyone, her heart had puddled in her chest. Her instincts were to reach out and pull him under her wing like she did all strays. She sensed a deep sadness in him. Maybe because she was sad, too.

If she had a hot man to heat up her sheets for a while, maybe she could forget about the deep chasm in her heart that refused to heal. Captain was just here for a few days. She couldn't keep him. No, this connection with him was about one hot night.

I'm definitely going to learn his moves.

"Ready to be blown away?" he asked, his hand on a door handle.

The sounds of music and people were coming from the other side of that door. She knew what she'd see when he opened it—the grand hall. The last time she'd been in there she'd danced with Matt during his seventeenth birthday party. Well, she was dancing and he was crunching her toes. She'd had to throw her sandals away after the party. Bruised toes and broken shoes hadn't mattered one bit because that night he'd told her he loved her.

Pressure built behind her eyes. *No. Stop. Matt is gone.*

"Julia?"

She let out a deep breath and fixed her harlot blouse. "Show me what you've got, Captain."

"That's my girl." He threw the doors open wide.

Five

"The music's getting loud downstairs." RW poured champagne into a crystal flute and handed it to Angel. "To you, my darling."

She clinked her glass with his water bottle. "To second chances."

He'd toast to that. She was his second chance, even if she didn't want to be. Couldn't be because she was his therapist. He'd never known what it felt like for someone to understand him, to see his inner demons and not run away.

Angel had saved his life, plain and simple, and now she pushed him toward the final phase of his therapy. Together they had hatched up an intricate plan designed to heal all the wounds created by his illness. He didn't think the plan would work, but for her, he would try.

After her first sip she asked, "Did they all come?"

"Chloe and Jeffrey arrived this morning. I haven't seen Matthew yet, but the staff tells me he's around. I'm waiting for him to make his presence known." RW tried to relax his fist. He was holding his bottle too tightly. The veins in his neck were pounding. "I'm sure however he chooses to arrive, it will be a showstopper."

"Give him time. He'll come around."

"Maybe. He's a Harper, after all. We're all a bit bullheaded."

"Don't I know it." She winked at him. Playful and sweet. He'd be lost without this woman.

"You've changed me. You see that now, don't you?"

She eyed him. "Well, you do look as handsome as a pirate."

Not what he meant. He wanted to press her, ask if she'd thought about his offer again. But his instincts said to wait and give her time to consider it. Consider them.

She drank the last of her champagne and put the glass on the marble table. "All right, pirate. Go down to your party. Just remember the plan. It'll work."

"What if it happens again?" He swallowed hard, not wanting to remember how he used to be, unable to stop.

She put a cool hand on his. "It won't."

When she smiled up at him, the gnawing, twisting thing in his gut eased. She was the only one who could calm him. With her by his side, he dared to believe he was ready to put the plan in motion and call his children home. He touched her bare shoulder with the back of his knuckle. God, she was so soft, so perfect. "Will you stay?"

"I shouldn't."

"Why? I invited the whole town. No one will put

two and two together. Plus, I bought the pirate costume for you. You'll be unrecognizable."

She rose up on her toes and kissed his cheek. "Can't take the chance."

The darkness swirled inside, yanking on him, trying to drag him under. His voice came out broken and raw. "I can't do this without you, Angel. Please."

RW Harper didn't beg but everything had changed when Angel came into his life.

Her gaze met his. He could only assume she saw his demons, the ones that had nearly killed him and all he loved. The ones she was fighting to destroy. That had to be the reason she dipped her head in affirmation. Because she didn't love him, couldn't love him. And soon, after the plan was complete, she'd leave.

If he didn't get stronger, that thought alone would end him.

Six

Julia gasped when Captain pulled her into the crowded hall. It looked the same as it had for Matt's birthday party ten years ago. Her chest squeezed so hard that breathing hurt. Everything ached. She felt small, ragged.

She pulled her hand from his. "I have to go."

He faced her and probably saw full-fledged anguish in her eyes. Instead of letting her go, he stepped into her space. He put his hands on her shoulders and said, "No one will hurt you here. I promise. Please stay."

He lied. She was already hurting, big-time. "You don't understand."

A trumpet blast made her jump. The band struck up a beat and the singers started in on one of her favorite songs.

"Think of the birds you want to save. Plus…" Captain crooked his finger at her. "I can't show you my moves if you won't step onto the dance floor with me."

She bit her lip. The plovers needed her. She did love this song.

And she wanted this man.

Julia gave him her hand and let him lead her in. "This song is really good for—"

He spun her under his arm. "Salsa. Relax, I've got this." And just like that she was dancing with a pirate.

Barely twenty seconds into the song, she realized she'd met her match. Everyone was watching, but Captain hadn't stopped watching her. It gave her a zing up her spine to be the focus of his attention.

"You dance well." She meant it as a compliment. So why did her voice dip with sorrow?

Because part of her wanted to believe that somehow Captain was Matt reincarnate. The way he danced destroyed all hope. Matt could barely move his feet to a beat while her date danced salsa like he'd had years of practice. He wasn't her boy. It was time to let Matt go for good and enjoy this hot man who'd dropped in for a night.

"You're not bad, either." He pulled her closer so her breasts pressed into his hard chest. "For a girl."

He grinned and she forgot about the past. She lost her mind. Those lips! She couldn't stop gazing at them.

Placing her hand on his jaw, she enjoyed the feel of his beard under her palm. He stopped dancing. He studied her intensely. Had the music slowed or had the world stopped moving? She didn't know. All she could focus on was the way he looked like he could make love to her right there on the dance floor.

And she wanted him, the past be damned.

She wrapped her arm around his neck and pulled his lips to hers. The kiss she gave him wasn't small or sweet. Her lips had been lonely for so long that they just took over.

Fire licked through her core and her heart pounded hard. She was overcome with need. For this man. Right now.

He held her cheeks and gave back as good as he got.

It wasn't enough. *More, more, more!* everything in her cried. She ran her tongue inside his mouth, tasting, exploring. The groan he made told her she was doing something right. One of his hands released her face and pressed into the small of her back, holding her to him, keeping her right where he wanted. She was breathing fast and burning up.

People around her disappeared. She completely forgot where she was, who she was, but she knew exactly what she wanted. *More!*

The taste of him, the way he kissed, made her head spin. His lips were perfect. They fit as if they were made for her. A fever of desire engulfed her.

Heaven help her, she wanted that hand on her back to move lower, to squeeze. *More, Matt!*

Matt?

She pulled back and blinked at Captain. What in the world? For just a second there she'd thought…but that wasn't possible.

When would her stupid head get it?

Captain's grin was gone, replaced by an intense expression that spoke volumes. He was as worked up by the kiss as she was. They were fully clothed and in public.

What moves would he show her when they were alone?

A slow, sensuous song started playing and he spun her around until her back was against his chest. He pressed one hand to her belly and they rocked together to the beat. Slowly, he ran his other hand up her arm, down, petting her skin. Every nerve cell she owned sizzled. He moved the hair of her wig and kissed her neck.

She gasped and closed her eyes.

He nibbled on her ear and pressed himself against her. "Feel how much I want you."

There was no doubt about what she was feeling. She swallowed hard and simply nodded.

While they rocked from side to side, his knees bumped her legs and he nibbled her ear. Waves of shivers rolled over her body. It felt so good. He made circles with the hand on her belly, dipping lower, lower…stopping too soon. She rolled her hips, trying to get those fingers where she needed them. She wanted him to cup her through the skirt, to hold her nice and tight. He was pushing all her buttons and there was no way to go back now. She wanted to cry out for more.

"Miss Espinoza, you have defied the restraining order," an authoritarian voice said behind her. "You need to come with us."

Julia's eyes flew open to see two guards surrounding them.

Captain growled, "Like hell she will."

"Sir, this is official business. Step back so no one gets hurt," the second guard said.

"Take her," the head guard said. Obeying, the other man grabbed her arm.

"Back the hell off!" Captain gave him a shove and

stepped in front of Julia, shielding her with his body. "Touch her again and someone *will* get hurt. I've waited a long time to settle a score with you two."

The first guard frowned and the second pulled out his gun. Several women screamed. Most of them were Julia's relatives and she couldn't let anyone get hurt.

"No!" Julia yelled. "Stop. I'll go with you. Just put that thing away."

Captain shook his head. "You're not going with these goons."

The head guard stepped forward. "Stay out of this or we'll have you both arrested."

"On what grounds?" Captain growled.

"Trespassing."

Captain laughed and then looked around the room, searching for…who? His gaze settled on someone Julia couldn't see behind Captain's big frame.

"Why didn't you fire these two jackasses already?" he asked.

The room went still. All eyes were on Captain.

Who was he?

After a few beats of silence, the head guard spoke up again. "I don't know what you're trying to pull, mister. But enough is enough." He reached for Julia, yanking her sleeve off her shoulder. She had to scramble to keep "her treasures" from popping out of the blouse, just as Tía Nona had predicted.

Captain took a swing and cold-cocked the guard. He was out before he hit the floor.

The other guard's eyes went wide. "Don't move!" He stepped forward with his gun aimed at Captain's chest.

"No!" Julia cried out.

But Captain didn't flinch. He actually said, "Drop it."

Julia was terrified his bravado was going to get him shot.

"Please, Captain. Let's just go," she begged.

He didn't move. "Stay behind me, sweetheart."

RW Harper's voice boomed. "What in the hell is going on here?"

Captain didn't turn or take his eye off the gun. "About time."

Julia's heart sank. Was Captain RW's partner or a friend? Whatever the case, he wasn't on her side if he was buddies with that monster.

"Speak!" RW demanded.

"You tell me, Dad. Why are you trying to have my ex-fiancée arrested?"

There was a collective gasp in the room.

Julia couldn't make a sound because she couldn't breathe. Couldn't see straight. Or think.

Dad? My ex-fiancée? The words didn't make sense. Her heart beat in her ears and her vision tunneled.

Air, I need air.

"Put the gun away," RW ordered. He turned his attention to Captain and, to Julia's utter surprise, he clapped the man on the back. RW was smiling so big that he looked like a different man. She'd never seen Mr. Harper when he was not angry. "Matthew! So glad you came home."

Matthew? She was weak; her legs wobbled.

Someone behind her clapped. Another followed suit. Applause, whistles and hoots filled the room, along with prayers of *"¡Gracias a Dios!"* and "It's a miracle!"

Julia couldn't speak. Her head pounded. Her throat closed.

After all these years, Matt is alive. Matt is...here.

Emotions, all of them, roared over her in a crashing wave. Debilitating. Short-circuiting her brain. It was more than she could take. She shoved her way through the crowd, through the kitchen, out the side door and into the night.

"Julia!" Matt yelled.

He wanted to go after her, but before he could register what was happening, RW hugged him. Matt didn't know what to do. The only form of touching he could remember his dad using was with fists. He stood dumbfounded, his hands at his sides as his dad squeezed.

"Thanks for coming home, son," RW said with genuine emotion as he released him.

No yelling. No slamming doors. This was a new world for Matt. He wasn't sure how to negotiate it. He started to run his hand through his hair but touched Henry's bandana instead. He pulled it off his head and tucked it in his pocket. "I have to talk to Julia."

RW nodded, more stiffly now. "Of course."

People blocked him, circling, all talking at once. Everyone tried to touch him as if he were a long-lost prince. Screw that, he had to find Julia. He lifted his eye patch so he could see better over their heads. *Where did she go?*

Mumbling his apologies, he strode around the group and was about to open the door to the kitchen when Maria, Julia's cousin, stepped into his path.

"You're Matt Harper?" Her hands were on her hips. Fury radiated off her frame. Her boyfriend stood behind her, looking menacing.

"Yep. I need to find—"

Maria took a swing and punched him in the eye.

"That's for breaking Julia's heart. Do it again and it'll be your balls. Come on, Jaime."

With his eye pouring water, he tried to make sense of the last five minutes. Breaking Julia's heart? How was he the bad guy here? Julia had gotten married and started a family without him. She'd chosen to block him from her memory. Hell, he'd never forget how the color had drained from her face when his dad had said his name.

Apparently, she'd really thought he was some stranger she'd picked up at Juanita's. That thought didn't sit well with him, since she was clearly turned on. By a stranger. The realization twisted in his gut while the rest of him still burned for her.

He couldn't think straight when she touched him. When she kissed him? Hell, he'd almost lost it. She'd never explored his mouth like that before. Little Julia had become a sexy, passionate woman. He'd wanted to take her home and kiss every inch of her body. Slowly. The way she'd pressed her sweet ass up against him had made him think she'd be up for the idea.

So why had she run?

He shoved his hands in his pockets and pulled out Henry's bandana. Only one thing left to do. He'd return what belonged to the kid and maybe get one last chance to clear the air with Henry's mother before flying away.

He didn't belong in Plunder Cove. Julia Espinoza had made that painfully obvious. He was no long-lost prince. He was a regular pilot who was wanted on the other side of the world.

Not here.

Seven

Angel watched Julia from behind the gazebo.

She wished she could run after her and stop the beautiful young woman from making the same mistakes Angel had made. How she ached to help the young lovers, but her hands had been tied long ago.

If she stepped out of the shadows, she'd be killed. Only RW knew her secrets and she trusted him with them since she knew his, but she had to be careful. Her own life mattered little when people she loved, especially Julia and Henry, could be hurt.

She couldn't risk it. She let Julia go.

Her cell phone buzzed in the pocket of her pirate dress. *"¿Hola?"*

"You knew, didn't you?" She'd been the brunt of Tía Nona's anger for so many years that she'd recognize the woman's voice anywhere. "Matthew Harper is alive."

Angel sighed. "I did know, yes."

She heard undecipherable Spanish swearing. "You'd think a person would've seen fit to tell me. I am Julia's guardian, after all."

Guardian? That was a stretch. Julia was a grown woman now. Nona should've pulled her nose out of Julia's business years ago. In truth, Julia was taking care of Nona and her sisters far more than they were taking care of her.

"This is between RW and his son. Julia moved on a long time ago."

"I don't give one *culo de rata* about RW and his son. Those two destroyed Julia. You weren't here then, so you don't know." That stung. Nona had a way of digging in and chomping down like a Chihuahua. "It was long ago, yes, but I haven't forgiven the Harpers. You shouldn't, either."

Angel had learned that forgiving RW had been easy once she truly understood him. His demons were brutal. She doubted she would've survived what he'd lived through. No, kindness was what RW needed. If she didn't have her own issues, she would take him up on his offer to stay, to love away his pains. Again, the choice wasn't hers.

Angel was a marked woman quickly running out of time. Forgiving RW, getting to know the real man inside the billionaire's shell, was a rare and special gift she hadn't expected. She'd offered to be his therapist in secret because she longed for her own redemption. She knew him better than he understood and felt his pain and loss as acutely as she'd felt her own. Others might've taken advantage of his fragile state for money or fame but she wouldn't hurt him. He'd made her feel almost whole, wanted. It was far more than she deserved.

She was the reason her family was in danger. She was to blame. Forgiving herself was the one thing she couldn't do. And she wouldn't stay with him just to feed her own desires.

"Julia has been sad for far too long. She deserves to feel joy and let her struggles go, even for one day. I hope you will let her have this, Nona."

Nona huffed. "We all want to be happy. Do we Pueblicitans have a say in the matter? We bow at RW's feet, scrape the crap off his boots and pretend to smile. He throws us a crust off his plate and we're supposed to treasure it as if it's a jewel out of his pirate's chest? You forget, I worked in that house for many years. I saw what sort of man he really is."

"He's changed," Angel said quietly.

"With you he is different, but how do you know he has really changed?"

She didn't know for sure, but she had hope, which was something the Pueblicitans lacked. The ancestors of the people in this town had been purchased as workers and the generations after them had been freed, but held down for so long that they'd forgotten how to hope, how to dream.

RW couldn't make up for all that they'd suffered. But he was going to repair as much damage as he could. Because he had changed. She refused to think otherwise.

"I better go. Maria and Jaime are taking Julia home. She should be there any minute."

"Good. She just needs time to adjust to having Matt home, alive. Please don't discourage her, she is a grown

woman with her own mind. Make sure she's okay and
then meet me at Juanita's. We've got a lot to discuss."

"That we do, *mujer*. My heart hasn't beat this hard
in a long time. Seeing him on the front porch tonight.
¡Híjole! I'm going to need tequila to help me sleep,"
Nona said.

Angel nodded. Why should tonight be any different? "Kiss Julia for me."

"I will."

She knew Nona wouldn't say the kiss was from her.
It broke her heart.

Matt hopped on his bike and sped off toward Julia's
house. He didn't take the long way this time. He roared
through the curves. He couldn't shake the feeling that
somehow dear old Dad had something to do with why
Julia seemed so shell-shocked. The sooner he spoke to
her and understood what in the hell was going on, the
sooner he could be done and fly out.

The lights were out at 3C Bougainvillea Lane. He
shut the bike down and softly rapped on the door. He
heard sniffling inside.

"Julia, it's me."

Nothing.

But she was there. He could almost feel her breathing.

"I need to talk to you." He pressed his forehead to
the door. "What has my father done?"

He was angry enough to pound his fist against the
wall, but he didn't want to wake her son. Instead he
pounded his own leg. She was driving him insane.

"Julia, you promised to love me forever once. Or
have you forgotten?"

She opened the door halfway. The wig was gone, so were the fishnet stockings. Her makeup had smeared under her eyes and she looked younger, more like the Julia he used to coax out of the house to sneak down to the beach for midnight skinny-dipping.

She was in a sheer nightgown with her beautiful, thick hair hanging over her shoulder. The one entry-way light bulb provided backlighting enough that he could see through her nightgown. It took everything in his power to keep from pushing the door open and sweeping her into his arms.

"I thought you were dead," she said, a mixture of what looked like pain and wonder pooled in her eyes.

He cocked his head. Who'd told her that? He didn't want to believe it. Instead he let himself express the hurt he'd felt at losing her. "Good to know you thought of me at all, sweetheart."

Confusion flashed in her eyes. "Why would you say that?"

He didn't touch her. She didn't come closer. "You moved on without me." He couldn't keep the bitterness out of his words.

"You didn't even say goodbye." He heard her anger, too.

"I wanted to." This was killing him. Being this close to her, laying his past bare. Accepting all that his father had done. Was it possible they'd both been manipulated? He softened his voice. "Listen, Julia, can we just talk?"

She blinked fast, as if she was about to cry. If she did, it would be game over for him. He'd hold her and never let her go.

Luckily, she beat back the tears and let loose a string

of Spanish words instead. Motioning to the sky and back to him, he could only catch and recognize a few of the phrases. Shaking her head, she focused on him.

He could feel her indecision, her desire, her... amazement?

"You were dead," she whispered, stepping into him. "Oh, God, Matt, I thought I'd lost you. " Her gaze was on his lips and tears dripped from her lashes.

That did it.

He swept her into his arms, needing to touch her, to taste her. The kiss she pressed to his lips was salty, not sweet. He returned it with heat and deep, raw craving.

It surprised him how much this hurt, kissing the woman he thought he'd never kiss again.

He'd lost her, too.

She wrapped her arms around his waist, holding on, as if worried he'd disappear.

His hands dove through her hair, cradling her head as he kissed her. Every part of him felt electrically charged. It was as if his cells were crawling out of an abyss. Crawling toward the sun. Toward Julia.

"Matt." She pulled her lips away. Her fingers touched her swollen lips before she asked, "What happened to your eye?"

He touched the bruised one. "I ran into a fist."

"Your father?"

"No. Another enraged relative. I'm fine. It's you and those small white birds I'm worried about."

She crossed her arms and raised an eyebrow. "The snowy plovers?"

"Yeah." She wasn't buying his line. Those birds were not why he was there and they both knew it. But he'd use whatever he could to keep her beside him, talking to him. "I promised to help you get that intel from the house and you left too soon. We could team up to save the plovers before I leave. Matt and Julia against the world, one last time."

"You're leaving Plunder Cove?"

What was that on her face? Disappointment?

He watched her body language—the way she leaned into him, her palm on his chest, how her gaze kept drifting to his lips. He held still, mesmerized by the tiny circles she was drawing with her fingers.

"I just got you back. I don't want you to go. Not yet." She let out a tiny breath.

That statement shouldn't make him as happy as it did. He fought to keep his lips from twitching upward.

"I was worried I'd forgotten how to…desire someone. I was dead, too," she continued. "But when you touched me—even though I couldn't believe it was you—all these feelings, sensations and heat bubbled up and made me…" She looked him in the eye. "You made me *want*."

His pulse kicked up.

"I haven't felt that in a long time. Didn't think I ever would. Please, Matt. Let me…feel."

"What do you need to feel?" He pressed his lips to her forehead, softly.

She seemed to savor the kiss before answering, "Alive."

He ran a knuckle down her soft cheek. "Oh, babe, you are the most alive person I know. Your spirit, your drive, your light. Those are the things that kept me going in battle."

"I'm not that girl anymore. I seem to have lost

those bits of myself. But maybe if you stay in Plunder Cove…"

A slice of despair tore through his chest. He wasn't staying. He couldn't.

"Julia, I have an airline to run. I'm leaving on Monday."

"I have you for the weekend, then. " She blushed, "I mean, if you don't have other…plans. The two of us can…I mean, if you want to…we could be together. For one last time, or for three…" She swallowed hard, not meeting his eyes.

He tipped her chin up so he could look in that amazing smoldering gaze of hers. "One last time or three?"

Her cheeks were bright pink but she nodded. "Four?"

He grinned. "Are you propositioning me, sweetheart?"

"Yes?"

"I heard the question mark. Try again."

She bit her lip but didn't continue.

"Say you want me to make love to you all weekend. Say you want me to kiss every bit of you. Tell me you want me to lick, suck, nibble and make you come four times—" he rubbed her arms, slowly deliberately "—in a single hour."

"Yes, please," she croaked.

He laughed—because she wanted him and he desired her. And maybe they could have something like that honeymoon they'd never had before he flew out of Plunder Cove for good.

She rushed into his arms and sealed their deal with her kisses on his neck. "Thank you. This will be the closure I've always needed. We can both use this time to help us move forward."

"Closure. Sure."

The words nearly stuck in his throat. It was the first time in his life that he felt disappointment while a beautiful woman kissed his neck. He wouldn't show it, or any of the other emotions he couldn't name. Not when Julia wanted him for hot sex.

He couldn't tell her why he hadn't said goodbye ten years ago, and he might not ever understand why she'd believed him to be dead. Those misunderstandings didn't really matter anymore. She'd married someone else. Had someone else's child. And he had his own dreams to fulfill, away from here.

They couldn't go back to what they'd once had. But maybe they could have this short time together.

She gave him a kiss on his chin. "Tomorrow."

He grinned. "We could start right now."

She smiled up at him. "No. Henry's inside and I have to go back to him." Gently, she petted Matt's jaw and cheek, as if she still couldn't believe it was him and really liked the feel of his beard. Her hands felt so good on him. She could put them all over his body. "Come by in the morning. I'll make you breakfast."

He kissed her long and slow. When he finally pulled back, he liked the soft and pliant Julia looking back at him. The anger was gone.

"I'll be here. Good night, Julia Espinoza."

Her lips turned up into a smile. "Good night, Matt Harper."

Then he watched her turn and go inside.

Eight

When he returned to Casa Larga, Matt was surprised the party was still going full-swing—until he remembered how much Julia's family liked to fiesta. He'd discovered it the hard way at Julia's *quinceañera*.

Her aunts had done things up right for Julia's fifteen-year-old coming of age party. They'd rented out the patio of a five-star resort in the closest big city. He'd worn his tux and waited in the parking lot for the rented limo to pull up, like everyone else.

The mariachi band had trumpeted in his ear when Julia had stepped out of the limo with a passel of girls trailing behind. She'd looked like a fairy princess in light pink and it had been hard to keep his tongue off the pavement. Her gaze had searched the crowd and found him. When she'd smiled at him, he'd thought he was the luckiest guy on the planet.

The food and drinks had started flowing and he'd learned everyone in her family danced. He'd kicked himself a thousand times that night for not being able to spin the fairy princess around the floor. Relegated to leaning against the wall, he'd watched his beautiful girl dance with everyone but him. That night, he'd sworn he'd learn to salsa if it killed him.

Now music pulsed inside Casa Larga, spilling out into the night. He could hear laughing and singing. He didn't go through the side entrance this time but walked right in. The two ape guards were no longer standing at the door. Was it too much to hope that they'd been sacked already?

"Matthew! Over here," RW's voice rang out. "We waited for you to make the announcement."

His old man was upstairs, sitting on a couch surrounded by two faces Matt hadn't seen in a long time. Jeff had been kicked out of the house right after Matt. At least Jeff got to go to an exclusive Hotel Management and Design school in New York, but sixteen was still too young to be booted out of the nest. Chloe, his baby sister, had gone to live with Mom in Santa Monica, or Malibu, or wherever Mom had moved to after that. He hadn't stayed in touch with either of them.

He climbed the stairs and grinned. "Old home week."

"Matt!" Chloe jumped to her feet and rushed to hug him. Her long blond hair was pulled back in a braid that dipped and swayed low across her back. Her face was as expressive and sparkling as it always had been.

He held her, marveling. She had to be twenty-four already. "I don't know who you are, lady, but you remind me of a little girl I once knew."

She playfully slapped his arm. "You never call!"

Shame roared through him. "Sorry. I'm bad with phones."

"Text me once in a while, dork." She kissed his cheek and whispered, "Saw you dancing with a gorgeous pirate. Please tell me it was Julia."

He whispered back, "It was Julia."

She clapped her hands in glee. "Knew it! Way to go, bro."

"Look what the night dragged in." Rising from the couch, Jeff offered his freckled hand. He was the ginger in the family.

Matt shook, noticing the firm grip. His brother definitely worked out in New York. "Wow, you've grown six inches, at least. You've almost caught up to your big brother."

"I grew seven and a half inches, and look again. I passed you, old man."

They stood nose-to-nose. Damn. Jeff was taller. "Huh, you wearing high heels? Three-inch girl's stilettos?"

Jeff socked him in the arm. "Nope."

Matt rubbed his arm. Why was he everyone's sparring bag? "You hit like the last girl who punched me."

"Yeah, I can see the bruise. How did you insult *her*?"

"I admitted to being a Harper."

Jeff nodded. "That explains the black eye."

Chloe threw her arms around both of them. "So good to see you guys! I missed you like crazy."

"Missed you, too, Fish." He used the old nickname. His sister used to like to swim and surf with her brothers. Man, she'd been fast in the water for a little kid.

Matt looked up to see RW watching the reunion. He had his hands shoved into his pockets and his eyes seemed rheumy, like he'd been drinking all night, but there was no glass in sight. And RW Harper didn't drink.

What'd happened to the proud, mean man Matt used to know?

"Hey, Dad. What announcement?" Matt said.

RW took that as his cue to come closer to the trio. Slowly.

"He hasn't told any of us," Jeff whispered. "I get the feeling it's bad."

"Maybe not," Chloe said hopefully. She'd always been the cheerful one in the family. He had no idea where she got it.

RW passed them and walked toward the railing. "Let's gather the troops."

Matt raised an eyebrow. Jeff shrugged. Chloe's gaze was on her father, her arms still wrapped around her brothers.

"Cut the music," RW called down to some guy in the crowd. When it was quiet, he lifted his voice and looked out over the gathering like a king on his thrown. "Thank you all for being here. A special thanks to my children for coming home."

Matt crossed his arms. *Home?* Casa Larga had stopped being that long ago. If it ever was.

RW continued. "Tonight, I will share with you a new Harper Industries project."

Uh-oh. Was this the snowy plover destruction project? He wished Julia was here to hear the announcement.

Everyone waited for RW to go on. "Casa Larga will

be upgraded into a five-star resort and spa. Complete with tennis courts, golf course and all the amenities high-end clientele would seek. It will benefit everyone in Plunder Cove."

Chloe's head swung toward Jeff's. Matt noticed the flash of interest in Jeff's blue eyes, too. Hotel management had been his thing before he'd gotten into the reality TV business. Now he was famous for critiquing the most elite of hotels on his show.

It was all interesting, but Matt didn't know how this news would benefit anyone or anything other than RW's bank account. The people downstairs started whispering among themselves, probably thinking the same thing. What had the Harpers ever given them? The townspeople had worked for the family for centuries and yet most of them were barely existing above California's poverty level.

"In gratitude for the work you and your families have done for me and my family over the centuries, twenty-five percent of the profits will be set aside for the townspeople of Pueblicito. My lawyers have already drawn up the contract. I suggest you elect a representative, or a board, to sign for you and handle the money." RW smiled. "It's going to be in the millions."

A roar went up in the hall. Matt stared at his father. It was the craziest thing he'd ever heard him say.

"Please enjoy the food and refreshments and stay as long as you'd like." RW turned back to his kids. "How'd I do?"

Matt shook his head. "Are you on meds?"

Chloe elbowed him in the ribs.

RW's smile fell. "Why would you say that?"

"You don't give money to charity, let alone a whole town."

RW straightened invisible wrinkles out of his perfectly pressed shirt. "It's time to give back, my son. I thought you'd be pleased."

Pleased? Maybe, if his dad actually went through with it. More than likely, RW was running some sort of scam and the people of Pueblicito would never see a dime.

"I've always thought this area should be better developed. You're going to need a good team for the hotel and restaurant renovation. Want me to provide some names?" Jeff said.

"I already have the one name I need." RW clapped Jeff on the back.

Jeff stepped back. "No. That's not happening."

RW spread his hands. "This is what you were trained for, my boy. When you were little you said you wanted to build a fancy hotel. Well, this is it. Don't you want to be the creator of the best resort and restaurant in North America?"

Matt could tell by the way the muscle in Jeff's square jaw tightened that he was thinking about it. *Watch out, bro. He's trying to suck you in.* For what purpose, Matt didn't know, but RW worked people over until he got what he wanted.

Jeff must've remembered that, too, because he said, "Can't do it, Dad. My show is really taking off. We just got signed for another year."

RW blew through his lips. "That ridiculous show where you go behind the scenes to reveal the dirt behind the top-rated hotels? It's sleazy and beneath your talent. You want to do that for the rest of your life, Jeffrey?"

Matt could see the telltale redness of anger under Jeff's collar. Soon his ears would be red, too. Leaning against the railing, Matt growled, "Way to step all over his career."

Chloe came to her brother's rescue. "Dad! *Secrets and Sheets* has really high ratings. All my friends love it. Plus…" She leaned into Jeff. "They think you're cute."

Jeff shook his head. "I don't really expect a guy like you would understand why hotels need good critics to keep them honest."

"Critic? They're calling you a *wannabe*, son. You shouldn't want to be anything other than what you were destined to become—great. That's what I desire for you. For all of you." RW's gaze fell on Matt and then Chloe. "And I am ready to give you what you need to fulfill your potential. All I ask in return is that you stay here in Plunder Cove to see it through in case I am…elsewhere."

"Elsewhere?" Chloe's voice cracked. "Where are you going?"

"I can't say, but it's important I get this project in order." RW smiled. "I have plans for all of you. Chloe, my sweet girl, you can use your Sports Science degree to be the athletic director at the family resort. You'll be wonderful at it. You can plan all the events and outings for the clients. Anything your heart desires."

Chloe's mouth opened and closed again as if she didn't know what to say. But Matt could see the glistening in her eyes. Of the three of them, Chloe was the one who belonged in Plunder Cove. A guy would have to be blind to not see how much she loved the place and her brothers. Blind, or mean. RW had sent her away, too, banished her from the kingdom just like he had her brothers. It must've broken her heart. It was just one more thing Matt would never forgive RW for.

"Hold up. What are you doing now, Fish?" Matt asked. "In your career, your life."

He grimaced. He should know the answer. Damn, why hadn't he kept in contact? He shouldn't have punished the messenger for the bad news about Julia's marriage. Besides, he suspected their mother had forced Chloe to write the letter that had exploded his world.

Chloe's face quirked. "You, uh, are not going to believe this. I'm sort of famous, too. In Hollywood, anyway."

Jeff wrapped his arm around her shoulders. "Yes, you are. Miss Yogi to the Stars."

Chloe laughed. "You've heard of me?"

Jeff laughed. "Who hasn't? My producer has been bugging me for an introduction. He's toying with an idea to start a show about you. I'll give you his card before I leave."

Matt quirked an eyebrow. "What's a yogi?"

Jeff shook his head. "Dude, you've never heard of yoga? Hot babes stretching, posing, tight butts. You need to get your head out of the clouds."

Chloe slugged Jeff in the arm. "It's more than sexy stretching, dork. Try my class and I'll introduce you to muscles you didn't know you had."

"I know where my muscles are." Jeff rubbed his arm. Apparently, he'd felt that punch.

Matt shrugged. "There's your answer, Dad. When you weren't looking, your three kids grew up and got lives. I'm starting an airline in Asia, which you knew already, since you are contributing a plane. I'm not staying around to…what? Fly in your billionaire clients?"

"Sounds like your childhood dream, doesn't it? Flying planes on your own schedule with time to ride your motorcycle, hang out with the locals and swim in the ocean." Strangely, RW did not seem perturbed or dissuaded. "Take the weekend to think about it. All of you."

Chloe raised one finger. "I, uh, don't need the weekend. I hate the fakeness of Hollywood. It's impossible to make real connections there. For the past ten years, I've wished we could be a real family again. If I have half a chance to work with my brothers…" She rose up on her toes and kissed Jeff's cheek and then Matt's. "I'm going to take it." She blew RW a kiss. "Thanks, Dad. Count me in."

"I'll stay until Monday but then I need to head back to New York. My *wannabe* show is poised to make millions. I'm not walking away. But I can find you some of the top men in the business for the renovation and hotel management," Jeff said.

"Sleep on it for a couple days." RW shifted his weight. "Perhaps you'll realize what an opportunity this is for you. For the family."

Matt narrowed his eyes. What was RW's evil scheme here? Whatever it was, he wasn't going to be controlled by his power-grubbing father. Been there, survived it, moving on.

"I'll stay the weekend. Must be something I can do to pass the time," Matt said.

It took lots of work to keep his grin from turning

into a full-fledged smile. Oh, he was going to do something, all right. Make that one sweet *someone*. Matt already had plans over the next couple of days.

Julia had voiced her needs and he'd promised to give her four orgasms in one hour. He couldn't wait to get started.

Nine

Julia woke, showered, put on a skirt and a lacy, pink T-shirt, scrubbed the kitchen counters and popped a Spanish frittata in the oven all before the sun came up.

Sexual frustration? Check. Nervous energy? Double check. Scared out of her mind? Triple check. Matt was coming to breakfast. Her Matt. How had he survived? Why hadn't he called her? Written?

What happened?

No, don't think, just enjoy it while it lasts.

Matt was in Plunder Cove alive and sexier than ever. And he was hers for one weekend.

Her heart pounded, thinking about their kisses last night and that dance. She was getting hot all over again. She rinsed a clean cloth under the faucet and pressed it to her forehead.

Henry shuffled out in his pajamas. "Mama?" He

rubbed his eyes. "Whatcha doing? Do you have a fever?"

Yes, yes, I do. The kind only Matt Harper can cause.

"I'm cleaning. Company's coming for breakfast."

"Who?"

"The pilot. We called him Captain last night. His real name is Matt."

"Sweet! He was cool."

She smiled and pressed his bed-hair down with the wet cloth. "Yep."

Matt Harper had always been the coolest guy she knew. She'd been smitten the day she'd met him when she was only twelve and he was thirteen. She and a couple of friends were hanging out at Juanita's, eating multicolored snow cones, when a cute boy with dark hair rode by on his dirt bike. He came back around, popping a wheelie in front of her.

"Show-off," one of the girls mumbled. "Look at him. Such a bad boy. Nothing but trouble."

Oh, she was looking, all right. "Who is he?"

The girl slurped juice out of her cone. "Just some boy who cleans up for Juanita. He acts like he owns the place."

The other girl snorted. "No duh! He does own the place. That's Matt Harper. You know, RW's son?"

"Really?" The girl's voice sounded different then. Like she was watching a prince pop wheelies.

Matt rode by again, this time with both of his hands behind his head and his gaze on Julia.

"Ooh, la, la. I think he likes you, Jules," the second girl teased. "Better wipe the shaved ice off your face. He's coming over."

She scrubbed the stickiness off her cheeks as Matt

came skidding in sideways in front of them. He had blue eyes and a grin that made her stomach dance.

"Wanna ride?" he asked her in a voice that slid over her skin, warming her icy lips.

One girl shook her wrist and snapped her fingers— the sign for H-O-T.

"Me?" Julia croaked.

"Yeah, you, beautiful." He grinned and her legs went wobbly. Her cheeks were on fire and something weird was happening in her stomach.

"Tía Nona will kill you, *chica*," the other girl said.

"Come on. I'll go slow." He was cute and seemed sincere.

She threw away her snow cone. "I don't know how to ride a bike."

He put his hand out. "Doesn't matter. I do."

She'd never held a boy's hand before. She took it and quickly climbed on the bicycle seat.

"Lift your feet a little and relax. I've got you." He stood and started pedaling.

She'd never trusted a stranger with her life before. Something about Matt Harper made her try. Since her own parents didn't want her, she doubted anyone else would. Until Matt Harper, the cutest bad boy in Plunder Cove, had singled her out for a ride.

He took her down to the beach and they went swimming. It was the single most fabulous day of her young life. Only to be followed by better days and nights with Matt Harper over the next four years. She'd given him her heart the moment she'd sat on his bicycle seat. They were just kids, but for the first time Julia knew what love was.

She gave everything she had to Matt Harper.

And he'd blown everything apart. She wouldn't make that mistake again. The broken shards left in her chest were not going to anyone but Henry—the son Matt didn't know he had and said he didn't want.

He'd told her more than once that he would never end up like RW and all the other bastard Harpers before him because he wasn't going to be a father.

But now that he was a father, should she tell him? Would he hate her for it?

Would he stay?

She shook her head.

Falling in love was a girlish dream that had no place in her life now. She'd have one last fun-filled weekend with Matt and let him go. Somehow.

He knocked on her door and she nearly jumped out of her skin.

"He's here!" Henry announced.

With her hand pressed against the bongo drums in her chest, she nodded. "Why don't you put on some real clothes and I'll let him in? Something clean!"

Henry raced off to his bedroom and she hustled to the door.

There Matt stood, with a bouquet of wildflowers in his hand, looking like the bad boy of her dreams. "Hi, beautiful."

The adjective didn't even begin to describe the man filling up her doorway. "Hi." The sound came out breathy.

She let her gaze travel from his intense blue eyes, over his full lips and square jaw. He wore a chain around his neck and a telltale bump under his T-shirt. *Interesting.* He still wore his dog tags. The black T-shirt pulling across his chest was much tighter than the pirate shirt he'd worn last night and it highlighted his broad shoulders and muscular arms.

He held still as she took him all in. Her hungry gaze traveled down his pecs, over each bump of his six-pack abs to his… Oh. He was aroused already.

He wasn't the only one.

She glanced over her shoulder to make sure Henry wasn't behind her and grabbed Matt by the front of his T-shirt and pulled. His lips crashed into hers. His frame—everything about him was large and hard— crashed into her, too. They fell back against the wall with a bang that she hoped seemed louder to her than it really was. If Henry ran in and saw her making out with a man in the kitchen, it would be…awkward. Since she could still hear her son ruffling through his drawers in his room, she ran her fingers through Matt's hair and kissed him for all he was worth.

He yanked the flowers she'd just smashed out from between them and held them over her head, caging her against the wall. His mouth lit her on fire. Her brain kept squealing, *I'm kissing him. This is real. Matt Harper came back!*

"Mama, is my Pokémon shirt clean?"

Move away from the hot pirate. She couldn't do this in front of Henry.

She wiggled out from under Matt and called out, "Doubt it. You wore it the last three days in a row."

"It's barely dirty," Henry whined. "Only has a few stains and doesn't smell like my socks. Can I wear it?"

"Find another, Pig-Pen." She motioned Matt inside her home. "Come."

"Nearly did, babe. I really liked your good-morning

kiss." He handed her the mangled bouquet. "I brought flowers."

She pressed her lips together but a smile snuck out. "Sorry, I'm a little…excited about our weekend."

He ran his knuckle down her neck and across her chest. "Me, too."

The heat! It was going to kill her. If they kept going like this, she'd combust or jump him again in her small kitchen.

"Not in front of Henry," she whispered to herself more than him.

"Okay, but that means you can't kiss me like that. Or look so damned sexy."

She looked sexy? She met his eyes and became lost in them. "I'll try not to."

He chuckled. "Sorry, sweetheart, but you're going to have to try harder. Looking at me like that turns me on."

She was turned on, too.

He winked. "I won't mess anything up between you and your son. I can sit on my hands, or something, maybe count from one thousand backward. You got any coffee made?"

"Yes, I've already had three cups."

"Three? You're drinking me under the table. What time did you get up this morning?"

"Two thirty. I couldn't sleep."

"I should've come over to start our breakfast date early." He rubbed her shoulders. Had he noticed how tense she was?

She gently touched his shiner. "I'm sorry. Maria told me what happened. She's pretty protective of me and does have a mean right hook. Does it hurt?"

He puffed up his chest. "This little thing? I've had worse."

She remembered bruises on his teenage body. It hurt her to think about what he'd been through.

"Hi!" Henry popped into the kitchen.

"Henry!" she said. The little rascal was shirtless.

He shrugged his skinny shoulders. "Can't find anything to wear."

"Doesn't bother me to see a pair of guns." Matt offered his hand and Henry pumped it like crazy. "See? Look at those muscles. Nearly ripped my arm out of the socket."

Henry laughed. "Maybe if you had bigger guns you'd be able to block a girl when she aims for your face."

"Henry! Don't be rude."

Henry's cheeks went red. "Sorry. Just kidding."

Matt smiled. "No problem. You're right. I need to work out more. But you should've seen the girl. She was really tough."

Henry giggled. "Yeah, you should see Tía Nona when she gets mad. Stay out of the way."

She poured Matt a cup of coffee and a glass of *horchata* for Henry.

Henry scratched his bare belly. "What happened to the flowers?"

Nice manners, kid of mine.

Matt shrugged. "They got a little messed up. Next time I'll pick sturdier ones that can take a real smashing."

Julia snorted and both pairs of eyes were on her. "I don't need flowers, Matt."

"I know. I just want to give you things."

Her eyes misted. "You already have. You're here."

Henry's gaze ping-ponged between the adults as he slurped his drink. "So, uh, how do you know my mama?"

Julia bit her lip, debating. Should she go for the moment of truth, or deflection?

Matt spoke up. "Your mom is…how do you say *sweetheart* in Spanish?"

Henry's eyebrows knit together and he cocked his head. "*Querida.* I think. Is that right, Mama?"

Julia nodded slowly, waiting to see if Henry understood the implications of the word.

"Care-ida." Matt completely butchered the word. His Spanish accent had always been terrible.

"Just stick to English, Matt. No offense but your accent—"

"Stinks." Henry waved his hand in front of his face. "Like really bad."

Matt laughed and ruffled Henry's hair. "Thanks a lot. Whose side are you on, anyway?"

"Smells worse than Mama's breakfast."

"What?" Julia jumped to her feet. Smoke was pouring out through the cracks of the old oven. "Oh, no! The baked frittata."

"Watch out, sweetheart." Matt motioned for her to step back. Taking the fire extinguisher off the wall, he opened the oven and pulled the trigger. Her baked frittata became a black charred mess covered in white foam.

"Oh, no." She let out a little cry. "Our breakfast."

Henry hugged her waist from the back. "It's okay, Mama. I hate that frittata thing. Especially the mushrooms."

"What? You always act like you like it."

Henry shook his head, the curl sticking up on the top of his head flipping back and forth. "Just, you know, didn't want you to get sad or anything over it."

"Mushrooms are not my thing, either, kid." Matt made a disgusted face.

Huh, she hadn't known that.

"I'm sure I would've loved your mom's but I messed it up with foam. So, I get to take you two out to breakfast. My treat." Matt took out his cell. "Give me a sec to call Alfred to bring one of the Batmobiles."

"Wait. You know Batman?" Henry asked. "I thought he was a made-up guy. Like SpongeBob."

Matt leaned closer and whispered, "Today, you get to be Robin."

"Woot!" Henry's fist pumped the air. "I'm going to put on my green shirt. If I can find it." He raced back to his room.

"Good luck with that. Maybe if you cleaned up your room once in a while." She leaned her head on Matt's shoulder. "Sorry. I had this whole meal planned for us, which apparently Henry hates."

Matt wrapped his arms around her and pulled her to his chest. "You don't have to cook for me, sweetheart. Let me take care of you. And that Henry…"

She momentarily stopped breathing waiting to hear what he'd say.

"…is a blast. Love that kid."

She pressed a hand to her heart. "You do?"

He kissed her forehead. "How could I not? He's just like his mom."

Her heart melted. He was wrong, of course. No kid alive had ever been so much like his father—her lips quirked—down to keeping mushroom-hating a secret so as to not hurt her feelings.

She wasn't going to tell Matt the truth about Henry. Not yet. It was better to wait and assess the situation. He used to say he didn't want kids after the terrible relationship with his own father. Henry was far too important to thrust on a man who wouldn't, or simply couldn't, love him. She'd rather keep his paternity a secret than have him get hurt. She didn't know her own father and that had worked out okay. Sort of.

Matt called the driver and she aired out her smoky kitchen. Standing on her tippy toes, she reached as high as she could to open the tiny window by the stove. Couldn't quite get it. Normally she used a step stool but didn't have time to go search for one. Trying one more time, she was startled to feel his hand on her butt.

"Need a lift?"

"Yes?" she squeaked.

He kept his hand where it was, rubbing and squeezing her glutes, while reaching the other over her head to open the window. She was still on her toes when he shifted and reached around and dragged his hand up her inner thigh. Slowly, he pulled up her skirt.

"Matt," she whispered. *Henry could come in any min*— Her thought was cut off when he cupped her through her panties.

Oh. That's...oh.

She swayed on her toes.

His free hand held her around the waist, locking her to him. "I've got you," he whispered in her ear, sending electric waves up her spine. "Don't. Move."

His hand held her in place. When his thumb started to rub, lightning bolts shot through her. She couldn't hold still. Her back arched against him. Her breathing came fast, hard. She gripped the countertop and started to rock.

"That's right, come for me, Julia. Let go."

She tipped her head back, resting on his chest. He released her waist and turned her head toward his. Taking her mouth, he plunged his tongue inside even as he continued the relentless rubbing. The lightning bolts went off everywhere. She cried into his mouth as the orgasm rolled through her, over her.

He pulled his hand out from under her skirt and just held her.

She blinked. What just happened? She'd never come so fast or felt anything like that before. She was still fully clothed. He was clothed, too. And yet that was…

"Amazing," she said in a voice she barely recognized. It was so breathy and came from a woman wholly satiated at 7:00 a.m.

"It doesn't count," Matt said.

"What?"

"It wasn't one of the four I promised you. I just had to touch you, that's all. Consider it a warm-up."

She swallowed hard. "Sure, that's, um, fine."

Fine? Could she be any more of a *tonta*? The man had just exploded her world in her own kitchen and it didn't count. What would he do next?

Henry came into the kitchen wearing his dark green shirt. "Found it! Will this work for Robin?"

Matt gripped Henry's shoulder. "Dude, you're the best-looking Boy Wonder I've ever seen. Alfred has brought the Batmobile to us."

Henry scrambled to look out the window. "Whoa. What kind of car is that?"

Matt peeked, too. "That, dear Robin, is an Aston Martin Rapide. It's not the most expensive car Mr. Harper owns, but it's not the cheapest, either. Want to sit up front?"

"Could I?" Henry looked at Matt and then her.

"Sure. Why not?" she replied.

Henry was out the door before she could change her mind.

"You okay?" Matt asked.

She held his gaze. "Better than okay. Matt, that was…" She didn't have the words to describe how he made her feel. And seeing him with Henry melted her insides.

"I can do better, I swear." He seemed so sincere, like a kid who'd run the race but didn't get his best time.

She lifted her eyebrow. "I'll hold you to it."

He rubbed his hands together, accepting the challenge as they followed Henry outside.

She nodded to the driver holding the door for her.

"Sir, where would you like to go?" the driver asked.

"Juanita's. She's got the best ham and eggs in a hundred-mile radius," Matt said. "Plus, I was sort of hoping to catch her."

"Juanita's? We could've walked there," Julia said.

"Yeah, but then Robin wouldn't get to ride shotgun and I wouldn't get to nibble on your earlobe in the back seat." He took her hand and laced her fingers with his.

She glanced at Henry. He was busily staring at all the technology in the car and asking the driver a hundred questions.

"Relax," Matt said.

She put her head on his shoulder and closed her eyes.

Ten

The driver dropped them off in front of Juanita's. Two old guys sitting out front admired the car.

"Do you want me to wait, Master Harper?" Alfred laid the formalities on thick for Henry's benefit.

"We'll walk back. Thanks."

Alfred started the engine. "That is a fine young man," he said, referencing Henry. "His mother raised him right."

Matt took an extra couple of seconds to watch Julia and her son walk up the sidewalk. Mostly arms and legs, Henry was a year or two from passing Julia in height. A few years after that he might turn into a hellion like most teenage boys do, but for now they were shoulder-to-shoulder and damned cute together. He wished he belonged in the picture.

Where the hell had that thought come from? He was

not here to create a family with Julia. This was a weekend of "closure," nothing more. Even so, he pulled out
his cell and snapped a memory he could keep forever.

He ran to catch up.

It was a warm summer morning with just the right
amount of ocean breeze in the air. They sat at a three-
person table outside. Before he put his cell phone on the
edge of the table he said, "Hey, can I take a picture?"

"A selfie?" Henry asked.

"Not just of me. Of the three of us." He looked into
Julia's eyes. She made a strange sound, like a choked
cry. She covered it with a cough. Followed by two long
sips of water.

"You okay?"

She nodded. Another sip. She wasn't okay but he
didn't press her.

Henry rubbed his hair down on the side. "I'm ready.
Take the picture!"

"Okay. Move in close." They both did and he tucked
them in under his arms. He stretched over Henry's head
and snapped another keeper.

"Made a fresh batch of churros. Not that any of you
would be interested." Juanita herself came up to their
table and deposited a plate of warm churros.

"No, we aren't interested. And that is not my tongue
hanging out." Matt grinned, rising to his feet. "Glad
to see you. I was worried I'd miss you before I left.
But mostly I worried you'd run out of churros." Teasing Juanita came naturally. She was the one person
on the planet, other than Julia, who let him be himself. Not RW Harper's son. Not a troublemaker. Not a
pilot. Just Matt.

"Really?" Juanita tsked. "In that case, you don't get

any. Here, Henry, these are all for you." She pushed the plate toward the kid.

"Whoa. Just kidding!" Matt lifted her off her feet and swung her around, kissing both cheeks before releasing her.

She cupped his face, her eyes misty. "Silly boy. Why'd you stay away so long?"

His gaze cut toward Julia. "Things happened."

Juanita scrunched her nose like she used to do. How was it that his old friend looked just the same? She was still a beautiful woman with thick dark hair and brown eyes that could see straight into a person and know when he was talking bull.

"Whatever happened, I'm happy to see you here, Matt Harper. You're looking good. All grown up. And still trouble."

Julia nodded. "Truer words never spoken."

Juanita pinned him with her gaze. "You are leaving soon?"

"In a few days. I have to get back to work."

"I see. That's a shame. Looks like you are right where you belong." Her voice was cloaked in meaning.

She had seen Matt fall in love with Julia from the beginning. More times than not, Matt had snuck out his bedroom window to secretly meet Julia right here, at this very table. Or at the back of the market where he could kiss her without anyone seeing. But Juanita had seen them and kept their secret. He would always love her for it.

To Henry she said, "I met this young man when he was about your age. He used to work for me and eat all my candy."

"The white ones? I like those the best," Henry hinted.

"Is that so? Perhaps I can find some for you to take home if you eat all of your breakfast."

"Woot!" Henry pumped the air. It seemed to be a favorite way to express his joy. Matt liked it.

"Woot!" He punched the air, too.

They both laughed and, without any thought, Matt lifted his hand at the exact same time Henry did. They high-fived each other across the table.

Julia's mouth fell open.

Juanita said softly, "*¡Dios mio!* It's like looking in a time-travel mirror."

"Excuse me." Julia pushed her chair back, making a scraping noise across the patio. She fast-walked through the café and market toward the restrooms.

"I'll be right back," Juanita said, following Julia.

Julia blew her nose and splashed water on her face. *Stop. This is not helping.* But the tears flowed anyway.

There was a knock on the door. "Julia? It's me. Can I come in?"

Sniffling, she unlocked the door and let Juanita in.

"Oh, *cariña.* This must be very hard on you. Seeing Matt after all these years." Juanita wrapped her arms around Julia.

Julia sobbed on the woman's shoulder. "That's not it." She blubbered. "I'm…happy. Really. It's seeing *them.* Together."

Juanita looked into Julia's face. Even through the tears, she could see the intensity in the woman's eyes searching into the depths of her heart. Juanita had a gift for drawing out a person's deepest feelings. "You haven't told him Henry is his son."

Julia couldn't answer. Tears flew off her cheeks when she shook her head.

Juanita pulled a paper towel out of the canister and dampened it. Gently she wiped Julia's tears. "Why not? That boy was smitten the first day he saw you. The look on his face is the same."

Juanita had always been such a kind person. Julia was grateful for the support now. She needed someone to talk to about this situation, preferably someone who wasn't a fist-throwing relative.

"He's leaving, Juanita. At the end of the weekend, he'll be gone. He's starting the life he always wanted on the other side of the world. I can't take that away from him."

Juanita frowned. "What if he wants to change everything? If you don't tell him the whole truth, he won't be able to make the right decision for himself. For all of you."

"What is the right decision?" Julia sighed. "I was so happy when I found out I was pregnant. A part of Matt grew inside me when I believed I'd lost him. That stinky little lovebug saved me. Gave me a future to live for. But I didn't have to think about how Matt would react to having a son. I didn't have to face his reaction. Now I do."

Juanita cocked her head. "Why wouldn't he be thrilled? Henry is the best kid around."

"He's not perfect. And it might not matter anyway." Anguish was a knot twisting around her throat. "Once, after a bad fight with his dad, Matt told me he never wanted kids because he refused to turn out like his dad. He was afraid that could really happen. And now

I just drop Henry on him? Surprise, you're a daddy! How can I do that to him? To Henry?"

"Matt might be happy about it," Juanita said. "Men grow up and change their minds."

"Or he could be furious or feel trapped. He's dreamed about being a pilot since he was five years old. That dream doesn't include me and Henry. What if leaving is the right thing for him?"

Julia shook her head. "I'm afraid. What if I tell him that he's a daddy and he feels forced to stay here out of a sense of duty? He'll lose his dream, his destiny. And he'll eventually hate me and Henry for it. It's not fair to him or my kid."

Juanita's pretty face was creased with sadness. "If Matt was a scary guy, I'd support your decision. I'd do everything I could to keep you and Henry safe. But we're talking about Matt here. You should give him a chance to be a great father. He's not RW. Never has been."

No, but could she risk everything on a pretty dream just because she wanted it to be true?

"I am going to be with him as much as I can this weekend and when it's over I'll let Matt decide his own path. If he stays, it's because he loves me and cares for my son. If he leaves—" she sucked in a deep breath "—I let him go. Please don't tell him about Henry."

Juanita's gaze searched her face one last time. "You sure?"

Not about anything. "Yes. That's the way it has to be."

Ana, the waitress, arrived, carrying all three dishes. "Pancakes with ham?"

"Yo!" Henry said.

"¿Machaca?"

"That's my girl's," Matt said, pointing to Julia. "No tomatoes. Corn tortillas. Side of guac."

Julia smiled. "You remembered."

"Of course. I remember everything you like." He hitched an eyebrow and she got all tingly inside. Again.

The waitress put the last plate down in front of Matt.

"*¿Lengua?*" Julia was shocked. "Since when?"

"Thought I'd order something different." He cut off a slice and held the forked meat in front of Henry's face. "Here, you try it first."

Henry shook his head. "Eeew. Cow's tongue? No way. That's a big n-o! Never eat something that tastes you while you taste it."

Matt burst out laughing. The rich baritone was music to her heart. Henry laughed, too, and the music became a symphony for her soul. For the first time in a decade, she had a glimpse of real happiness.

It terrified her. She didn't know if it was scary because it was only temporary or because she wanted it so desperately.

Matt brought the meat to her lips. "You try it."

Lengua wasn't her favorite, but she opened her mouth and let him in. She chewed slowly, deliberately, her gaze pinning him. She swallowed and licked the corner of her mouth. "Yum."

She saw the moment his teasing expression turned to desire. His pupils dilated. His breathing changed.

He cleared his throat and turned back to his meal. "All right, kid, here we go." Matt cut off another slice and chewed. "Well. It doesn't taste like chicken. Not too bad, but I think I'll stick with ham next time."

The waitress came to check on them and stayed to chat. "Did you guys hear what happened at the Harpers' last night? Everyone's talking about it. *¡Híjole!* I'm going to buy a new car with my share of the money. I can't believe it. How about you?"

Matt shifted in his chair uncomfortably. "I wouldn't count on that money."

Ana frowned. "Why not?"

Julia tugged on his arm. "What's this about?"

Matt softly said, "I'll tell you later."

The waitress would not be deterred. "Mr. Harper is going to turn the old mansion into a luxury resort and give the townspeople a share of the profits. Millions! That's what he said. I've had my eye on a cute red Mazda. Can't wait to call her mine."

Matt didn't look happy. "Yeah. Well. I'd wait to cash the check before you go car shopping."

"Millions!" Henry spoke up. "That's a lot."

"It's not happening," Matt said.

"That's not what Mr. Harper said." Ana crossed her arms. "He should know."

"Exactly. Can you remember the last time Harpers gave you money other than wages? A tip, even?"

The truth sank in. "Thanks a lot." The waitress threw up her hands. "The first good thing happening to this town in forever and you…you…" The rest of the words were in Spanish, punctuated by the stomping of her boots as she walked away.

Matt pinched the bridge of his nose. "Do I dare ask what she said?"

"Something about the killer of pretty car dreams," Henry interpreted. "So? What are we going to do with our money? Can we buy a plane? I want to fly like my daddy did."

Matt's head lifted. "Your dad was a pilot, too?"

Julia sighed. She could not go there now. "Tell us about the money."

"That's just it. There is no money for anyone except for RW Harper. Pirates never change." Matt sounded more resigned than angry.

Henry looked crushed.

Matt put his hand on his shoulder. "Sorry, kid. But I know this guy well enough to tell you he doesn't pay anyone more than he should. If he can cheat or pay less, he will. He's selfish that way. At least we know he's not out to kill off the snowy plovers. That's a good thing, right?"

Henry pouted. "I guess."

"How do we know that?" Julia asked. "RW may want to use that patch of beach where the plovers lay their eggs for a snack bar or Jet Ski launch, or who knows what? We need to find out exactly what he's planning, Matt."

"I agree, sweetheart. This whole thing smells like bad news to me. First, he boots his children out of the kingdom and goes underground for years, then he pops up announcing he's paying people he's despised his whole life. And everyone buys it?"

His voice was getting loud. She touched his knee under the table and he let out deep breath. "I just don't get it. Why do people believe him? You know what he's like."

She did remember. "I don't believe him," she said. Not after the way he'd treated his son. She would never forgive Mr. Harper for hurting Matt.

Henry put his elbows on the table. "Me, neither."

Matt nodded. "Okay. Let's figure things out so that no one gets hurt."

"Like real crime fighters!" Henry said.

Matt high-fived him. "Yes, sir. A team." He took her hand and put it on top of theirs. "The three of us."

It was all she could do to keep her bottom lip from quivering. God, she wanted the three of them to be a team.

As they left the café, a car pulled up next to them and a woman leaned out the window. "Ooh, la, la. It's the salsa dancers."

Julia waved. "Hi, Linda."

Henry ran around to the back of the car to talk to his second cousins.

Linda acted like she'd swallowed a canary. "I took your red dress to the cleaner. Should be ready for you to wear tonight."

"Tonight?" Julia asked.

"*Sí, chica.* My mother says she wants to get a better look at your man. Come to dinner tonight. My place."

Matt wrapped his arm around her. "We'd love to. Thanks."

She shot him a look. "Don't we have other plans?"

"We do, yes. Major plans, before and after dinner." Now Matt had swallowed the canary.

"Mama, can I go over to Linda's house and ride bikes?" Henry asked.

"If Linda agrees."

"No *problema.* I'll keep an eye on him while you two…" She wiggled her eyebrows. "Do *before* dinner."

Julia's face was even hotter.

"Thanks, Linda. We'll come over around six?"

Linda winked. "*¡Hasta luego!* Get in the car, Henry."

"'Bye, Mom."

"Be good," she said. And the car drove away.

Matt pulled her closer. "Now I have you all to my-self." He kissed her in broad daylight on the sidewalk in the middle of town. As if it was a natural thing to do.

As if he would kiss her like that forever.

She never knew a heart could beat faster and shatter at the same time.

Eleven

They stopped by her house and picked up a few things.

"Don't forget your bathing suit," Matt said. "I've commandeered the pool house as my temporary digs. It's as far away from RW as I can get while still being on the grounds."

Her lips quirked. "Since when did we ever need suits?"

"Ah, babe. If it were up to me, we'd run around naked all the time. But my sis and brother are visiting and might be in the pool, too. Better keep things PG-rated, at least outside. Inside…" He kissed the nape of her neck. "That's another story."

She shivered, liking the sound of that.

They strapped on their helmets and Julia wrapped her arms around his strong back. They rode Matt's bike back to Casa Larga.

Once there, he led her straight to the kitchen. "Going to need sustenance."

The kitchen staff seemed to love having Matt home. They prepared a tray full of fruits, nuts, crackers and prosciutto. He grabbed two bottles of sparkling water. "And hydration."

She blushed, wondering how strenuous the *before* dinner events were going to be.

He led her back outside and through the gardens to the pool. Someone was swimming laps, her strokes long and graceful.

Matt clapped. "Fish has been practicing. Bet she'd beat me in the 50-meter now." He leaned over the water and called, "Chloe!"

The figure did a flip turn and swam over to the edge of the pool where Matt and Julia were standing. When she removed her goggles, her blue eyes went wide.

"Julia!" Chloe said. "Oh, my gosh! It's wonderful to see you. I'm sorry I didn't get to say hello at the party last night. My brother had you otherwise occupied."

Had everyone seen them dirty dancing?

"Nice to see you, too. How's the water?" She changed the subject as quickly as possible.

"Come in. It's perfect."

"Okay. I'll put on my suit."

Matt pointed to the pool house while he put the tray of food on a table in the shade. "You'll find towels and sunblock in the bathroom."

She ventured inside a pool house that was three times larger than her home. Heck, it was larger than any home in Pueblicito. It came complete with a kitchen, large-screen television, a wet bar and a pool table. She couldn't understand how the boy who enjoyed sweeping Juanita's, fixing his dirt bikes and hanging out with the locals came from a home like this. It boggled her mind *anyone* lived like this. Wealth was as unfamiliar to her as having parents.

She felt like she needed to tiptoe toward the bathroom. When she passed his bedroom, she stopped. Her hand went to her chest. There on his nightstand was a picture of the two of them in the silver heart frame she'd given him for Christmas years ago. She'd scrawled "Love, Your Julia" with a silver sparkly calligraphy pen.

He kept their picture by his bed?

It had to mean something. She dared not hope too hard. Matt wasn't going to choose her, not when his career waited for him. It might have been his father who'd lied about Matt's death, but it had been Matt who hadn't said goodbye or made contact with her. It was Matt who hated to be in Plunder Cove for more than a weekend. It was Matt who couldn't stand to be in the same house, the same town, with his father.

Nope. Better to be realistic here and accept the worst before it hit. She was flying high now, but the fall was coming and it was going to do more than knock the wind out of her. She might not be able to get up this time.

Now that she knew Matt was alive but had chosen to leave her…how would she move on?

She forced her feet to take her into the bathroom to change.

Matt put his swim trunks on in the shower stall by the pool.

Chloe got into the hot tub. "So? You two look as happy as you ever were."

Matt grimaced. "Yeah."

He jumped into the hot tub, splashing his sister. Water sloshed over the waterfall into the pool.

"Hey!" She splashed him back. "I heard a sour note in your voice. What's going on?"

He tipped his head toward the sun. "She's in love with someone else."

"No. Who?"

"Her dead husband. You know, the guy you wrote about while I was getting my ass handed to me in boot camp?"

It was her turn to grimace. "Oh, wow, that was a hard letter to write. Mom made me do it. She said you needed to know and it would help you in the long run. Did it?"

"It gutted me."

Tears welled in her eyes. She reached out and touched his shoulder. "I'm so sorry."

As always, he pushed the pain down in his chest, trying to ignore it. "Not your fault."

"So, her husband died?"

"Yes, he was a pilot. Can you believe that? What are the odds we'd both be in Afghanistan and only one of us make it out alive?" *Apparently the wrong one came back to her.* "She has a son. He's amazing."

"Wow. I had no idea. What are you going to do?"

"Spend the weekend with her. And then leave while I still can."

"Leave? Why don't you stay and remind her how good you two are together?"

His throat constricted. "I lost her a long time ago. I can't stay here with a woman who can't love me—"

The sliding-glass door opened and Julia stepped out.

"Later," he warned Chloe.

When his sister smiled that way, he knew she wasn't going to give up. The Harper gene was strong in that one. "Let me help," Chloe said softly.

No. He didn't need help. He needed a fast plane to get him out of town. That was what he thought until Julia dropped the towel and Matt forgot to breathe.

"Hey, gorgeous." Her legs were long, her hips and thighs were perfectly proportioned. Her tummy was a little softer than he remembered and her hips had a sexy womanly spread. Simply gorgeous.

Julia eased herself into the hot water.

"I'm just going to get warm and then you two can have the hot tub all to yourselves. Wouldn't want to be the third wheel," Chloe said.

"You're not…" Matt was busy devouring Julia with his eyes.

Chloe laughed. "Yes. I can see that. I'm going."

"Wait. Will you take a picture of us?" Matt dried his hands off on his towel and handed Chloe his phone.

"Of course. It's good to have memories."

Matt wrapped his arm around Julia, pulling her close to him on the step. Julia planted a kiss on his cheek and Chloe smiled before heading into the house. They were still holding one another. Steam rose off their bodies.

"Are you ready to have another warm-up?"

"Another…?" Her voice was high, breathy. Just like he liked it.

"We've got to practice a bit before we work up to four in an hour. You can't rush these things."

Before she could make another sound, he pressed his lips to hers and dragged them both under.

Twelve

She'd never been kissed underwater in a hot tub before. With Matt's lips on hers, who needed to breathe? He pulled her up. His hands ran down her shoulders and back. Water poured off her skin. Grabbing her butt, he yanked her closer so that she could feel exactly what was hard under the water.

"I want you bad, Julia." He nibbled her ear. That was bad and so good. "Let's go inside the pool house. I want to touch and kiss every bit of you. I'll pay special attention to what you like so I can do it all over again."

She had a feeling she was going to like whatever he did. Swallowing hard, she said, "When do I get to do those things to you?"

He ran his knuckle across her collarbones. "Babe, I'm yours. Whatever you want to do to me, with me, I'm game."

She licked her lips. "What in the heck are we waiting for?"

"I like the way you think." He all but hauled her out of the hot tub. He grabbed a towel and dried her off, slowly, sensually. The thick cotton smelled good and felt even better. When he got to her bathing suit bottom, she gasped.

"Like that?"

"Matthew Harper, take me to your bed before I throw you down and have my way with you right here!"

His eyebrow lifted. "I'd like to see you try."

She gave him a half-hearted shove.

On the way to the pool house, he snagged the tray of food and the two bottles of water. He popped a red grape into her mouth. "Blood sugar. Gotta keep it up for what comes next."

"Lots of promises, Harper. Show me the goods."

He playfully swatted her butt. "Oh, I'll show you, babe. Prepare yourself, because this is all I could think about since we danced last night."

Good to hear she wasn't the only one.

He placed the tray on his nightstand next to the silver heart picture frame. Their young, smiling faces and her scrawling love note was there as if he wanted her to notice.

What did it prove? That he still had those feelings? It was impossible. She wasn't that young girl anymore.

"I'm surprised you kept that," she said quietly.

He sat on the edge of the bed and patted the navy blue comforter for her to join him. "Why?"

She sat next to him, her arm touching his. "It was a long time ago."

"Sometimes it feels like just last summer. Except

last summer I was doing sorties in the Middle East." He ran his finger down her shoulder and leaned in close. He smelled like a mixture of chlorine and the musk she loved.

He made circles on her bare shoulder, dipping underneath the strap of her bathing suit. "Back then I'd wake up and stare at this picture, wondering how I got so lucky. I couldn't believe you were 'my Julia.' Let alone that you could love me. There's something I never told you…" He gazed into her eyes, the expression in those deep baby blues apologetic, serious. "I should've told you, it might have changed things."

"What is it?"

"You were the first person who ever said that to me." His lips tried to smile but didn't quite make it. "And the last."

She swallowed hard. "Your parents never told you they loved you?" No other woman had, either?

He laughed. It was the same humorless sound he used to make when people told him he was lucky to be a Harper. Was it possible she was the only person who'd ever said she loved him? Even Tía Nona told her that on occasion. Her cousins did, too. Henry said it every night when she tucked him in. If nothing else, Julia always knew she was loved. People cared.

Her heart tore. "I…I don't know what to say."

He shrugged, as if he could toss the sadness off his broad shoulders. "What's to say? You taught me what love is, Julia. Before then? All I knew was psychological and verbal warfare. My parents never loved each another. Maybe they didn't know how. Or they were both too stubborn to try. They taught us kids how relationships can turn toxic and ugly. They destroyed my family."

When he was a teen, he hadn't talked about the hell he was living in. RW was tough, but Matt's mother was a nasty, cold, overbearing woman who had a particular dislike for Latinas. Juanita had told her things and Tía Nona had confirmed them. Matt? Not so much. He'd just show up at her bedroom window, clearly upset, and start kissing her. She was sort of okay with it because... hot kissing, but she'd wished she knew how to help him. Even as a young girl, she knew that talking about what bothered or hurt her made things better. Matt couldn't or hadn't known how to share his feelings back then. But he was doing a pretty good job of it now.

He made a cracker-and-cheese sandwich and handed it to her. "Eat."

Holding the cracker sandwich in her hand she said, "Your father was hard on you. I saw the bruises and I didn't say anything. Now that I'm an adult, I know that was wrong. I should've called the cops."

"It wouldn't have done much good. He paid their salaries." He munched on a piece of cheese.

"I could've gone to the authorities outside Plunder Cove. Someone like...like..." She waved the cracker in circles, unsure who she would've contacted.

"The governor? A congressman? RW pays them all with donations. Don't worry, babe. You didn't do anything wrong. Besides, you were a teenager, too. Who would've believed us?"

It didn't ease her guilt. She took a bite and chewed solemnly.

He draped his arm over her shoulder. "Seriously, he wasn't bad all the time. I held my own with RW, mostly." He pulled her closer and took a breath, as if making a decision. "I gave in when he found the one way to control me."

She pulled a few grapes off the vine and popped one in his mouth. He kissed the palm of her hand. It was far more delicious than the snacks. "One way?"

"He had intel." Matt ran his hand through his wet hair, seeming to choose his words carefully. "Information that could've hurt your family. He threatened to release it."

"What kind of information?" That monster had used *her* to control his own son?

He didn't look her in the eye. "I don't know. Do you?"

"Me?" An idea niggled at the back of her thoughts. *Did RW know something about her parents? Were they in jail? Criminals? Dead?*

"It was probably a lie," he continued, "but I couldn't risk it. Harpers are good at manipulation. Must be part of the pirate gene. But my dad wasn't as brutal as my mom. That's why I've never wanted kids. What if I became like them?"

"You're nothing like them."

What would he say if she told him Henry was his son? Would he continue with his plans to leave Plunder Cove?

Would he stay?

Emotions, so many of them—confusion, grief and anger—mixed into a burning pressure behind her eyes. Rubbing his glorious, muscular back, she held her tongue.

"My parents took a lot of their frustrations out on me. I know that now, but as a kid, I only worried about two things. Keeping the damned information about your family safe, whatever it was, and protecting my brother and sister. I took their punishments, even when I wasn't at fault. I had to. Jeff and Chloe were so young and I was strong enough to take it because I had you."

Tears ran down her face.

He wiped her cheeks with his warm hands. "I had no idea the other side existed. Goodness? Kindness? Love and family? Those were words that had no meaning until you showed me the light. I'm so damned grateful to you, Julia." He kissed her shoulder, sending delicious shivers through her belly. And now…" He kissed her neck. "You are mine again for the weekend." His voice was husky and deep. "My sexy, gorgeous woman."

That was it. She kissed him hard.

Their warm, damp bodies collided. Matt fell backward on the comforter, pulling her on top of him. The tray of food went flying, scattering grapes and crackers across the bed. He held her against him as she did her best to devour his lips. His tongue pressed inside her mouth and hers rushed to meet him. He sucked on the tip of her tongue and she nearly had an orgasm right there.

Her hands roamed over his naked chest, shoulders, biceps. She wanted to touch him everywhere.

"You are so big," she said.

He grinned. "Why, thank you." His penis twitched as if she'd spoken directly to it.

She rolled her eyes. "I meant your muscles." She played with the hair on his chest. When he'd left her years ago, he'd only had a small patch. Now he had beautiful dark hair on his chest and a sexy V running into his shorts. She squeezed his right biceps. "And your height. You grew so much. I'm pretty much the same size."

He cupped her breast. "I beg to differ. You grew in all the right places." He reached behind her head and untied the top part of her suit. "Let me look at you."

It was unnerving to straddle him while his gaze took a nice, easy stroll over her. She forced herself to breathe normally, to act casually, and not to pull the covers over herself. She knew she was heavier than he remembered. Her belly was softer. Her hips had spread a little during the pregnancy. Her breasts were heavier, too.

"Julia. You are so damned beautiful."

He lifted himself up with his toned abs and took one of her nipples in his mouth. Pleasure shocks rolled through her. She arched her back and pressed into his hard-on. He sucked and a moan ripped out of her.

"You like that?" He rolled his tongue around her nipple. The cool air and the wetness combined to give her goose bumps. The good kind. Closing his eyes, he tugged gently. It drove her wild. She bucked on him, rolling over his engorged penis.

"Oh, babe. That's good."

He sucked on the other nipple and the moan turned into a small, begging cry. Everything about her screamed for more. He reached around her and wiggled his fingers under her swimsuit bottoms. As he sucked, he dipped a finger inside her.

Her mouth opened. She was all but panting.

"Matt, I want you." Her voice was husky, laced with need.

He kissed the side of her breast. "You have me,

Julia." That long finger was dipping in, out and waking up places in her that had been asleep for years.

"That's…oh. That feels amazing." She bit her lip. Where'd he learn to do *that*? "Um, no. I want you naked and inside…ahhh."

He laughed. "Just hold your horses, woman. I've got this."

Boy, did he. His thumb joined the party and pressed against her most sensitive spot. The finger tugged, the thumb pressed in tiny circles, and she was lost in glorious sensations. She tossed her head back and held on to his shoulders as electrified waves sparked and rolled through her.

"That's it, babe. So beautiful." His voice was full of awe.

Her closed eyes flew open when he held her waist and flipped her over. He kissed her, sucking on her bottom lip. Her body hummed.

"Your turn."

"Not so fast. We've got time."

Except we don't. A day and a half from now he would be gone.

"Matt! Take your swim trunks off already." She started untying the string to his striped board shorts.

He lifted his finger. "Patience."

And then he started nuzzling her belly. His beard felt so good on her skin. He kissed his way down past her belly button. When he got to her hip bones she wiggled.

"Still ticklish, I see." He nibbled gently and she squirmed.

"Matt…"

He kept kissing until his lips hit the waistband of

her bathing suit. She expected him to take her suit off but instead he kissed her through the fabric. The sensation of his warm mouth sucking through the cold, damp suit brought her to the brink again.

She moaned.

In one mighty tug, he pulled the suit down past her knees. Lifting her legs over his head, he paid a little attention to her petite feet. "Nice red polish." He rested her feet on his back. The suit locked her legs in place.

He stared at her bareness as if he was looking at a chest full of treasure. Gently, he opened her and ran his tongue over the silky skin. She gasped.

"You like that?"

She nodded. She'd never felt anything like it.

He did it again, slowly, deliberately. She almost couldn't breathe.

His tongue flicked her nub and her back arched again. Electricity shooting up from the base of her spine. She was so close. Again.

He sucked and the world exploded.

Thirteen

Pure magic.

Hell, why had he always been in such a hurry when he was a teen? He should've taken his time to really enjoy her soft, sweet-smelling body. To think he could have memorized the texture of her skin, the shades of her body—the pretty pink especially—and replayed those pictures in his head all those lonely nights in the Air Force...

Why hadn't he stopped to listen to the sounds Julia made when she felt good? What an idiot he'd been. Making her happy was worth far more than getting laid. He just hadn't gotten it as a kid. Watching Julia come undone in his hands now was by far the most beautiful thing he'd ever witnessed. He couldn't imagine anything more important. More pure.

He wanted to do it again.

He kissed her hip bone once more, only this time she didn't fidget. Was she too spent to be ticklish? He made his way back up and kissed her lips. Her eyes were closed but her mouth was turned up in the sweetest smile.

"I want to take your picture. Just like this," he whispered in her ear.

Her eyes were still closed but she was able to say, "Don't you dare."

"Matt! You in there? Whoa!" Jeff stopped in the doorway, getting an eyeful before Julia could scramble to pull the sheet around both of them.

Matt said, "This is not a good time."

"Yeah, I got that. I thought you were alone." He covered his eyes. "I want to talk to you."

Matt threw a pillow at his brother before he rolled off Julia and covered her completely with the sheet. She pulled it over her head.

"Everyone decent now?" Jeff peeked.

Matt crossed his arms. "Can this wait?"

"No, not really." Jeff leaned against the door frame. "We need to figure this thing out before you leave Plunder Cove. I'm afraid the old man is losing it."

Matt let out a deep breath. "Fine. Grab a beer from the fridge and I'll be out in a minute," Matt growled and Jeff closed the door behind him.

Matt pulled the sheet off Julia's face and kissed her pink cheek. "Should I kill him?"

"No. But I didn't get to, um, kiss you like you did to me. That was the first time… I liked what you did. A lot."

She was really blushing now. No one had ever gone down on her before?

"Ah, babe. There's plenty more where that came from. I was just getting started."

"More?" It came out squeaky. "But you didn't get to…you know."

He kissed the tip of her nose. "Later. We've got plenty of time for me. But if you want me to send my little brother away, I will."

"Little? Jeffrey is huge."

"Watch it, sweetheart," he warned. "I only want you to think about my bigness." He was still hard.

She chewed her lip as if indecisive. "You promise we'll have more time today for ourselves?"

"I promise."

She nodded. "You should talk to your brother." She needed time to recover and to get her emotions in check. "He might know what you father is planning. Besides, Jeff acted like he really wanted some brother time with you." She pressed her forehead to his. "Until later."

He gave Julia time to get dressed while he padded barefoot out to the game room to meet Jeff, buttoning his favorite Hawaiian shirt as he went.

Jeff offered Matt a beer from the game room mini-fridge. "Sorry, bro. I had no idea she was here."

Matt hoisted himself up to sit on the counter. He popped open his beer.

"Picking up where you two left off, huh?"

Matt looked around the corner. The bedroom door was closed and Julia was still getting dressed.

"It's just a weekend thing." A lump grew in his throat. He gulped his beer to force it down.

"You sure? Didn't look like it when you two were dancing last night. Sure didn't seem like it just now."

"She's got her life here, going to law school and raising her boy. Her goals and dreams don't include me. And mine don't include staying here."

Jeff studied him. "Huh."

"What's that mean?"

"It means you're fooling yourself if you think she doesn't want you."

No, he wasn't fooling himself. Julia wanted him, just not the way a part of him wished she would. She still mourned her dead husband and he *would* be a fool to think she felt that way about him after all these years apart. If his parents had taught him one thing, it was to not stick around for people who didn't care.

If he changed all his plans, if he stayed...it would only eat at them both until they hated each other. No. Hell, no. He wouldn't do that to Julia or to Henry.

Matt couldn't stay with a woman who could never really be his.

He ran his hand through his hair. "Why were you looking for me?"

"Change of subject. Okay, I get it." Jeff started chalking the pool sticks. "Doesn't it bother you that our father is not acting like himself? Opening up the family home as a resort might make sense if he hadn't been a recluse for the past few years. Now it's just weird. Giving profits away to the neighbors? That's insane. Plus, what did he mean that he might not be around to see it through? Chloe thinks he's dying."

Matt rubbed his beard. "This is RW we're talking about. He's too damned stubborn to die."

Jeff frowned. "What do you think he's up to?"

"A con. I don't know what or how, but he's doing what he's always done—using people to make money."

Jeff cocked his head. "He's using us?"

Matt laughed. All these years and his brother still didn't know how manipulative their father was? "Yeah, man. Always."

Jeff frowned. "Something about him is…different."

"Listen, Jeff. He booted us out of the house. I was dragged off to the Air Force academy and you were sent to the other side of the nation to go to boarding school. Chloe was sent to live with that witch we call 'Mother.' I swear Chloe got the worst deal. RW doesn't care about us. Never has. Don't let him get inside your head." Matt drank his beer.

"And now he's brought us back. Why?"

Matt shrugged. "Million-dollar question."

Jeff was silent for a moment, sipping his beer.

Matt glanced around the corner again. Still no Julia. Was she ever coming out of there?

"I want to ask you something," Matt said quietly. "Did RW ever mention information he had on Julia's family? Something that could destroy them?"

Jeff's eyebrow raised. "No. Is that what he had on you? I assumed you and Julia would elope or something. I couldn't figure out why you went into the Air Force instead. I always thought if I had someone to love me like you did…" He lifted his hands. "Hell, Matt. I would never give her up. I'd fight."

What his little brother didn't know was that he'd given her up to save her from his father. "RW gave me an ultimatum. I could leave or he'd release the information he had against Julia's family. He isn't known to make idle threats."

"Bastard."

Matt raised his bottle in agreement.

Jeff's brow creased. "What could it have been?"

"Julia never knew her parents. I wondered if RW dug up something incriminating on them. I didn't want RW to hurt her. So, yeah, I left."

"You went into the military to protect this girl." Jeff grinned. "Are you sure it's just a weekend thing?"

The door opened and Julia walked out. She was dressed in her cream-colored short pants and pink T-shirt. The sandals she wore had large, sparkly, fake gems and a sexy heel. Those red-polished toenails really got to him. Her eyes met his and a secret, sexy message passed between them.

Hell, he wanted her so bad.

"I thought you guys would be playing pool already," she said.

"Nah. We waited for you." Matt jumped down from the counter and took her hand. He laced his fingers with hers and drew her close. She'd pulled her damp hair up in a band she must have brought with her. He took one of the loose tendrils at her neck and coiled it around his finger. "I like the ponytail."

"We were waiting? I thought you'd lost your nerve and forfeited," Jeff said.

"Dude, you are so going down." Matt rolled his finger through the air. "Rack 'em up."

Jeff broke first and sent two balls into the holes at opposite ends of the table.

"Damn, you did learn a thing or two out there in New York." Matt laughed. "Glad I didn't put any money on this game."

Jeff bent over and took his next shot. "Left pocket." The ball did as it was told.

Matt wrapped his arm around Julia. "Good thing I have you to keep me company. Looks like I'm not going to get to play this game."

"Did you ask Jeff about the snowy plovers?" she asked.

Jeff looked up. "The what?" The next ball was an impossible hook shot that he easily sank.

"Julia thinks RW is going to build on the sand and wipe out endangered birds. Have you heard anything about his building plans for the resort or know how we can get our hands on them?"

Jeff straightened. "I told Dad I'd hook him up with a project contractor. The guy is coming in tomorrow afternoon. I'll see what information I can get from him and let you know."

"That's great, Jeff. Thanks."

"And if Dad's plans do include that section where the endangered birds are? What then?" Jeff asked.

"Then I nail him to the wall. Threat of jail time, fines, public humiliation. I won't quit until he does." Julia's smile was triumphant. "Couldn't happen to a more deserving guy."

Matt kissed her cheek. "That's my girl."

Fourteen

"Rematch!" Jeff called out the second after Matt sank the winning ball.

"You always were a competitive little squirt." Matt socked Jeff in the shoulder while winking at Julia. That man was clearly proud of his pool skills.

She blew him a kiss.

"And you need glasses, old man." Jeff returned the punch to Matt's biceps, only harder. "I haven't been a little squirt for years."

"Old man? I'm only fifteen months older than you. But I agree, I am way wiser."

Jeff snorted. "Really? Who got in trouble for breaking Mom's Ming vase?"

Matt crossed his arms. "You broke that thing? I thought Chloe did it."

Jeff leaned against the pool table. "We both did. I

was teaching her how to throw a curveball down the hallway and bam!" He smashed his fist into his palm. "Sorry you got busted for it."

Matt played with the black ball, ricocheting it across the table. "No biggie."

Suddenly, Jeff's voice seemed to thicken. "You said that all the time, Matt. But you're wrong."

Matt cocked his head. "About?"

"It was big stuff. I deserved far more than I got. Unless they caught me red-handed, you took it on yourself to protect me. You stepped into the fire for Chloe, too. Especially when Mom was on the warpath. You were—are—a great big brother. I never told you…oh, screw it." Jeff pulled Matt into a bear hug and muttered against Matt's shoulder, "Thank you, man."

Julia could see Matt's expression shift from cocky pool winner to being touched by his brother's words. Patting Jeff's back in that way men did, he mumbled, "Yeah, no problem." But she could see the emotion in his eyes. "You're a good brother, too. Don't beat yourself up over the past. It's not worth it."

All these years they'd never told each other how they felt? Tears welled in her eyes. She was witnessing an intensely private moment between brothers and was honored they'd let her see it.

She stole around the counter, snagged Matt's cell phone and snapped a picture of the two brothers hugging. *Memories*. She wanted Matt to keep this one forever.

"What do you say? Another game?" Jeff asked. His voice cracked with emotion.

"Depends on Julia. Do we have other plans?"

Like taking him in the back room? That would

be her choice, especially after seeing the way he responded to his brother's words. The vulnerable side of such a strong man was one of the sexiest things she'd ever seen. Matt was a good brother and had been a protector. Wouldn't he do the same thing for his own son?

If she told him.

But the two brothers were having a moment and she didn't want to ruin this opportunity for bonding between them. "One more game. I don't know how to play, but I like watching."

Matt racked the balls, giving her plenty to watch. His behind was perfection in those board shorts.

"I bet no one taught you the correct way to play." Jeff pointed his comment toward his brother. "I call Julia on my team."

"What?" Matt growled. "No one calls my girl."

Jeff shrugged. "Just did."

"Oh, no, Jeff. I'll make you lose," Julia said.

"You are my secret weapon." Jeff's grin was smug as he chalked his stick. "Go ahead, gorgeous, you go first."

"Um, okay." She took the pool cue, aimed, and shot the tip of the stick up and over the white ball. "Oops."

"Let me show you." Matt came up behind her, put his hands on her hips and adjusted her stance. She felt those big hands through her capris and her body started to hum. She shot him a look over her shoulder that meant, "After this game, I'm going to love you so hard."

He uncurled her fingers from the cue and kissed her palm. Gentle. Sweet.

Oh, wow, I'm not going to make it through this game.

"Make a little bridge with your hand like this. Push

your fingers gently into the cloth. Good. Head straight. Don't favor your dominant eye or you will be looking at the shot sideways. Nope. You're still tilting your head." He put his hands on her cheeks, straightening her head for her. The warmth of his palms felt so good on her skin. Too good. She was starting to ache again. How would she be able to think straight let alone hit the silly ball?

"And relax," he whispered in her ear.

Sure, easy for you to say, sexy man.

He was too close. She'd never be able to concentrate with him touching her like that. And he wasn't moving away, either. She could feel Matt's breath on the back of her neck, lifting the hairs that had come loose from her ponytail. She really would make Jeff lose. "Back up, Matt. You're impeding her shot," Jeff said.

"I'm helping her," Matt said confidently. "Right, sweetheart?"

Helping me to combust. "Sure. Helping."

Only one thing to do…she bent at the waist a little more and wiggled her fanny against him.

His sharp intake of breath told her she'd hit her mark. She rolled her hips from side to side and took her shot. Miracle of miracles, the ball went in the hole.

"Woohoo! Did you see that?" She spun around to face him and he grabbed her. He backed her hips into the edge of the pool table and kissed the thoughts out of her brain. Those lips of his made her feel like she was floating. But Matt had her pinned so she wouldn't fall. One hand was on her low back, pressing her to him, the other had started to run through her hair.

"Stop distracting my teammate." Jeff's voice pierced the wet, hot haze she was flying in. "It's still her turn."

She pulled the corner of her lips away from Matt's and mumbled for him to take the shot.

"If you say so." Jeff laughed. She heard the crack of balls dispersing across the table and the distinctive clunk of one going in the hole. Followed by another shot. Another clunk. Matt's lips lifted her higher again until she lost count of how many balls Jeff had sunk. She soon forgot Jeff was in the room.

Matt pulled his lips away but kept his hands on her. "My turn yet?" He gave her a slow, hot look.

"I won!" Jeff called out. "I mean, we won. I knew you'd be my secret weapon, Julia."

Matt narrowed his eyes. "You used a sexy woman to distract me? That's dirty pool."

"Ah, no. That's what you two were doing. Get a room already." Jeff grinned.

"I have one. You're in it," Matt said.

"Yeah, okay, I'm outta here. Nice playing with you, Julia." He gave her a high five.

"That was fun." She kissed Jeff's cheek. "Thanks for being a good brother."

His lips quirked and his ears turned pink. He didn't say anything as he put his pool cue away. But on his way out the sliding-glass door he said, "Matt, don't be an idiot. Don't let go. Fight."

The door closed and she was alone with Matt again. Her heart pounded in her chest.

"Don't let go?" she asked.

For a brief moment she saw a flash of anguish twist in the depths of his blue eyes. He pressed his forehead to hers and cupped her cheek. The muscle in his jaw flexed. He exhaled slowly. "Julia—"

Just then a cheerful tune played in Matt's bedroom.

She startled. "Where's my cell phone? That's Henry's ringtone."

She scrambled to find her phone while two questions played in her head.

What had Matt been about to say? Was he letting her go already?

She found her phone and checked the message. Matt leaned against the door frame with his arms crossed, watching her.

"Everything okay?"

She bit her lip. "I'm sorry, I have to go. Henry is on his way home now and I don't like him to be home alone."

"Okay, let's go. We can come back here after dinner. We have time."

Sadness swirled in her chest. Time was the one thing they didn't have. They had the past and a little bit of the present. Tomorrow was coming much too quickly and she didn't know what to do about it.

Several hours later, with Henry fed and occupied with his favorite TV show, Julia had showered, cleaned up and was now standing in her bedroom in her robe.

Her cousins sat on her bed, braiding each other's hair.

"What am I going to wear?" She wanted to dress up for Matt. If this was one of their last nights together, she wanted to wear something he would remember.

"The red dress, *chica*." Linda said. "It will *slay* him. I'm not kidding. My Jorge was so smitten when he saw me in it last night, I think we made another kid."

"Your ex is back?"

"Not really, just...you know, benefits."

Julia shivered. "You had the dress cleaned?"

"Clean and sparkly. Not one sequin fell off. Trust me, you will kill Matt right where he stands."

"I don't want to kill him," she said.

No, I want to seduce him and make all of his dreams come true. Maybe then he won't leave.

She swallowed the dryness in her throat. Where had that thought come from? She fought against it.

"I just want one fun weekend. You know, fun, just like you two are constantly harping on? 'Let the stress go, Julia. Have fun, Julia.' Tonight is about *fun*. It's not about asking Matt to stay. I have plans. Big plans. I'm going to be a lawyer, dammit. I will make RW pay for what he did to me, to you, to Matt, to all of us."

Her cousins were staring at her like she'd completely flipped.

Maybe she had. Her boyfriend had returned from the dead and introduced her to the best orgasms she'd ever had without even getting undressed and now he was leaving. What part of that made any sense?

"Don't you mean you're going to be a lawyer to save the birds?" Maria said softly.

Julia opened her mouth. Closed it. Her cheeks were suddenly very warm.

"Yeah, *chica*. Isn't your law degree about saving the planet? Tell me you are not on some vendetta to crush RW. You'll never win that battle," Linda said.

"Well, of course it's about saving the birds!" she huffed.

But was it? Her college education was for her and her son's futures. It wasn't about RW; it couldn't be. He had no power in her life. She wouldn't allow it.

And yet retribution sounded so sweet...

"So…? Are you wearing the dress or not?" Linda asked.

Julia blinked. "You really think he'll like it on me?"

They both nodded.

"Maybe it will be enough to get him to stay," Linda said softly, echoing the words Julia hadn't meant to say out loud.

She swallowed hard. Yes, Matt Harper was a flight risk. She'd be a fool to hope that he would drop roots in Plunder Cove.

"I see it in your eyes. I will snap him in two if he breaks your heart again," Maria proclaimed. "I swear I will."

"There will be no violence." Julia shook her finger, pulling herself together, tamping down her emotions. "I just want to enjoy him while he's here. Whatever happens, happens."

Maria grinned. "There it is. Did you see it?"

"Bright as day. *Ay ay ay!* She's done the nasty with him already. Maybe you don't need the red dress."

Julia could feel her cheeks burn. She tossed her hair out of her eyes. "How could you tell what we did just by looking at me?"

Maria shook her head. "We couldn't. Until now. We knew you wouldn't talk unless we tricked you into spilling the beans."

Linda laughed. "Totally busted. Good thing Tía Nona didn't catch you. That woman scares the crap out of me."

Julia crossed her arms. She and Matt were adults who were fully capable of doing…adult things. Tía Nona would simply have to accept that Julia was in charge of her own sexuality. It wasn't like she hadn't had sex before. Obviously. She had a child, for heaven's sake. "Tía Nona isn't the boss of me."

"I heard my name." Tía Nona came into the room. "Catch you doing what?"

Julia gulped.

Her cousins laughed so hard that they nearly fell off her bed. Julia shot them both a dirty look.

"You look nice, Tía Nona. Are you going out?"

"You think you're the only one invited for dinner tonight? I can't wait to talk to your 'Captain' to find out what he's been up to."

Oh, no. No, that can't be.

Julia had been planning to slip out with Matt after dinner. Linda was keeping Henry for the night, so Julia and Matt could pick up where they'd left off this afternoon. How would she slip away under her aunt's watchful eagle eyes?

"You're going, too?" Julia's voice skipped up an octave at the end. Like a kid caught stealing. Linda and Maria heard the squeak and covered their mouths to keep from laughing harder.

"I am going to slay both of you," Julia huffed and walked out of her own bedroom.

Fifteen

RW sat at his desk in the den studying the Harper Industries' quarterly report. So far, so good. The stocks were up, crude oil was holding its own and no one had figured out that he was a complete fraud.

Good news, all things considered.

There was a rap on the door. He rose quickly, hoping Angel had returned. "Come in."

He couldn't hide his disappointment when his bodyguard stepped into the room. "I have news, sir. The private investigator in Los Angeles has located a mole inside the gang. Someone who should be able to give us more information."

"That is excellent news. Who is it?"

"A woman named Cristina Sanchez. She came forward because Angel saved her life long ago, keeping her safe on the streets."

RW smiled. Of course Angel had saved her. His sweet, gentle Angel had a way of protecting and healing strays. Wasn't he living proof of that?

"Cristina says the gang is agitated again. She doesn't know why, but fears they have a new lead on Angel's whereabouts. The PI also noted that they've been packing up and getting ready to move. Should I tell Angel, sir?"

"No. Absolutely not."

If Angel thought her ex was coming for her, she'd flee again. RW might never find her. She needed *his* protection now. One way or another, he would save the woman who'd saved him.

"I want you to beef up the security around Plunder Cove. Men on boats monitoring the coast. Two in the lookout. Teams north and south. If anyone suspicious comes anywhere near Plunder Cove, you stop them. Hear me? No one gets within a mile of Angel. No one. If that bastard sends his entire gang after her, we will be ready. Understood?"

"Yes, sir."

"Good. Let's hope the mole will give us something we can use."

It was about time something went his way. He was going to do everything in his power to make Angel feel safe here in his home and maybe, just maybe, she would agree to stay.

Matt wandered into the kitchen and opened the massive double-doored refrigerator to peek inside. There were cheeses, fruits, spreads—it was like a mini grocery store in there.

"Matthew! Whatcha looking for?" Donna, the cook, called out.

She was standing over the stove, stirring a large pot of something that smelled good. That same short white bob still curled under her chin like it used to. Pushing seventy now, she wore red-rimmed glasses and orthopedic shoes, but she still had a youthful spunk to her steps. She was a kind and generous woman with a round, cherublike face and an infectious smile.

He closed the doors and went to her. Wrapping his arm around her shoulder, he peeked into the pot. "Mmm. This! What is it? It smells good."

"Wild boar stew. Sit. It's almost ready. I'll give you a bowl in a few minutes."

"Great. I'm starved." He hitched himself up onto the countertop and swung his legs like a kid.

"What else is new? I was told you were going out to dinner tonight."

"I am. But I can't wait until then." He held his stomach. "I'm dying here, Donna."

She walked to the fridge and pulled out a bowl. "I've got hard-boiled eggs, too. Want one?"

"How about two?"

"Growing boy." She smiled, handing him the whole bowl, and went back to stirring the stew. "Just like old times, huh? So good to have you back."

"Thanks. Not exactly like old times. I don't think I'd still be here if it was." He cracked an egg and started peeling off the shell. "Brown eggs?"

"Yes, we have a chicken coop around the back now. And an herb garden. We've gone to organic foods as much as possible after your father was ill."

He frowned. "Dad was sick?"

Donna stopped stirring. Her back stiffened but she didn't turn to face him. "You didn't know?"

"No. What was wrong with him? Is he still sick?"

Just then Alfred walked into the kitchen. "Perhaps you should ask your father about this, Matthew. We wouldn't want to speak out of turn."

Matt shook his head. "Communication between me and RW? That's not going to happen. Who is going to tell me what's going on?"

Donna turned slowly and he could see the concern on her face. "Now, Matt, we don't want to worry you, but your father has had some…well, troubles. He wasn't himself."

"You mean he was an even bigger jerk than he usually is? Donna, did he hurt any of you?"

"No! That's not what I mean." She looked at the driver. "Help. I don't know how to say this. Should I say this?"

Alfred let out a deep exhale that whistled through his nose. "Wait."

He looked around the corner and pulled the kitchen door closed. "Okay. They're still upstairs."

Who?

Alfred leaned against the countertop next to Matt's leg. "The divorce was very hard on your father. And even before that, when your parents were fighting, that was hard on him, too."

"When weren't they fighting?" Matt grumbled.

"Yes. But things got worse after you left. You weren't here to see how bad."

"That's when the illness really started to show," Donna pitched in.

He ran his hand through his hair. What the hell were these two trying to tell him?

"Spit it out, Alfred. The suspense is killing me."

"Your father had Harper Industries to run. No one could know how bad things were. How sick he was," Alfred said slowly. "If competitors found out, it would have been the end of Harper Industries. Your father could've lost the company his father and his grandfather and all the generations of Harper men had worked so hard to build."

"If they found out what?" Matt asked.

Donna walked around the counter until Matt was surrounded. It was as if they were trying to form a protective shield around him to ward off whatever bad news they were having trouble sharing.

"Your father," Alfred said quietly, "had a mental breakdown."

Matt blinked. "He what?"

Donna nodded. "RW went stark raving mad."

It was a sledgehammer to the solar plexus.

Matt had no words. He swung his head from Alfred to Donna and back again. When he finally found air in his lungs, he mumbled, "That's not possible."

Donna rubbed his arm. Her usual cherubic face was paler, stricken. "It's been truly horrible. He was slipping for quite a while but hid it pretty well. No one knew how much he was hurting. I doubt you kids had any clue."

"Hell, guys. Are you sure you're talking about RW? My father? The toughest SOB in California?"

Alfred moved back and cracked a boiled egg for himself. "Tough doesn't always mean strong."

Donna nodded. "That's exactly right. And RW had

to be strong for the family, the company and you kids. I'm sorry to say this, Matthew, but your mother was not an easy woman to live with."

Matt snorted. "Understatement of the year."

"They were bad for one another," Alfred said quietly. "As we now understand. The only good that came out of their union was you three kids. For that, your father is proud, even if he couldn't show it."

"Absolutely. RW was proud of you. In his own way. That's why all of this was so hard for him. He didn't want his problems to sink your future."

The air in the kitchen was suddenly laced with foreboding. Matt had a good sense of when danger was coming. He didn't always avoid it, but he could usually tell when it was heading his way. That sense had served him well in the Air Force. It was telling him now to get the hell out of the kitchen.

The chef and driver he loved were trying to feed him one of RW's lines of bull.

Matt pressed the headache that started burrowing between his eyes. RW didn't have a mental illness. Impossible. "I'm sorry, but I have to call this bull. I don't know why RW is tricking you like this, but there has to be a reason. He's not mentally ill."

Donna's face looked a little brighter. "Oh, you're right. He is better now, thanks to Angel. She nursed him back to health. Without her, I don't think he would've made it. Your mother was not the nurse type. She filed for a divorce when things got really tough."

No surprise there, but...

"Who the hell is Angel?"

"His savior. She was the only one who knew what to do because she'd apparently had some hard times

herself. Private woman, that one. Anyway, she knew
how to speak to RW in just the right way. We were
lucky she happened to be in town. Otherwise your father might have been institutionalized. Imagine what
a field day the press would have had with that news.
Angel stayed with him. Helped him get stronger. And
because of her kindness, he is better. You saw him. He
looks great, right?"

Great was not the way he'd ever describe his old
man. He was a good-looking guy, sure, but Matt no
longer looked up to him. Until he was old enough to
know better, he might have believed that his father was
a great man, but that ship had sailed and wasn't coming back. A great man protects his kids, tries to make
sure they are happy, secure and on the path to healthy
futures. RW did none of those things. Still, the man
Matt had seen at the party was not the same one who'd
yanked him up by the collar and ordered him to "shape
up or ship out."

Matt hadn't been able to put his finger on it, but he'd
sensed that his father was different.

"Tell me. What did he do?" Matt said.

Donna and Alfred glanced at each other.

"He wanted to protect you," Donna said softly.
"That's why he sent you away."

"Nope. Not buying it. He booted my ass to the Air
Force academy to keep me away from Julia. He told
her I died! That wasn't protection. That was being overbearing. He wanted to break us up because she was
from Pueblicito. My parents hated that, especially my
mom. And now I hate them for destroying the one good
and beautiful thing I had."

He scooted off the countertop and started pacing.

What in the hell was this crap? Had the old con artist bamboozled his staff into feeling sorry for him? Donna and Alfred should've seen through RW's tricks a long time ago. Was Matt the only one who knew what a terror RW could be?

"That's only part of the story, Matthew. Listen to Donna," Alfred said. "She saw the whole thing."

He spun and faced her. "What whole thing?"

"Do you know why your father didn't take you to the Air Force academy himself?" she said carefully, like she was wrapping cotton around each syllable to soften the coming blow.

"Haven't we already determined that he's an ass? It was easier to pay two men to dump his kid than to do it himself."

"He was incapable of taking you. That morning when I went up to bring him his coffee, I found him on the floor..." Donna tipped her head to the ceiling, struggling with the memory. "He'd taken pills, Matthew. Painkillers from a little vial. All of them. Your father tried to commit suicide."

And just like that, Matt's whole world slipped on its axis. The burrowing headache went off like a grenade. His body went weak. He blinked back tears he didn't know he had.

A voice that barely sounded like his rumbled across the back of his throat, "You're going to have to start at the beginning."

Matt turned up the second street in Pueblicito. The story Alfred and Donna had told him bounced inside his head. Shock waves were still rocking through his bones.

RW was mentally ill? He couldn't believe it and yet it explained a lot. Maybe he'd been such a hard-ass because he didn't know how to deal with his emotions… his life. Not to mention his crappy marriage. Matt's mother had a way of pushing everyone to the brink.

Matt parked in front of the fifth house on the street. It looked identical to the last four lined up in a row, except this one had kids' bikes piled in the front yard and music blasting inside. The only home in the whole town that stood out was the one Julia and Henry lived in. Julia had added pretty touches inside and out, making it a real home. If he lived here, he'd do his best to make sure Pueblicito got the upgrades it needed. Maybe those upgrades would come from the vast fortune his father was donating.

Matt rolled his eyes at the thought. Mental illness or no, his father was not so far gone that he'd give away money.

And I don't live here.

He had to keep reminding himself that his future was elsewhere. He was only a tourist having one last vacation.

He re-tucked his white shirt. His black shoes had been shined to perfection and his pants had been pressed because he wanted to look good for Julia. He'd even shaved off his beard. His palms were sweating when he knocked on the door.

Linda opened it. "You made it, *guapo*. Julia, Prince Charming is here."

Henry ran out to meet him first, bouncing and bobbing with energy. "Hey, did Alfred bring the Batmobile so I can show it off to the guys? They don't believe me that I got to ride in an Aston Martin Rapide."

Matt grinned. "Nope. I brought it myself. But it's not the Aston Martin." He cocked his head. "Take a look."

Henry peeked around Matt's elbow. His eyes grew wide. "Whoa. What is that?"

"It's a Lamborghini Veneno. If you promise not to put a scratch on it, I'll let you sit in it."

Henry's eyes were bugging out. "Are you serious?"

"I'd never lie to Robin. Just make sure you tell your buddies that it's not just any Lambo. Only three of these bad boys were ever sold."

"Really? Oh, wow. Guys! Get out here!" Henry yelled back inside the house. Then he turned around and hugged Matt around the waist. "Thank you."

It was the second time he'd been surprise bro-hugged in one day. He was starting to like it. He patted Henry's skinny back. "No problem."

Sure, RW might kill him for letting a passel of boys climb all over his Lamborghini, but the trouble was worth it to see the kid smile like that.

Julia stepped out on the porch in a low-cut dress. It was the same deep red that she'd painted on her toenails. Her dark, thick hair was draped over one shoulder. The hungry look in her eyes could not in any dimension compare to the ache filling his insides. He nearly died where he stood.

If he grabbed her up now, fireman-style, and carried her over his shoulder, he could run and maybe no one would notice.

She stared at him a beat too long, not moving, not speaking.

"You okay?" he asked.

"You shaved."

"I wanted to look respectable for you."

Touching his cheek, she let her cool fingers run along his jawline. Her hands were shaky and her lip quivered.

He took her arms. "You going to cry? It'll grow back. I promise."

"No, it's just…you look like my Matt again." Damned if a tear didn't roll down her cheek.

Her Matt. His heart pounded. "That's a bad thing?" He was treading on a thin precipice here. One wrong step and he was done for.

"No, not bad. You took my breath away. I'm being silly." She dabbed at her eyes. "Too emotional. Don't know what's wrong with me."

He laced her fingers with his. "I don't mind emotion, Julia. You can cry if you want. At least it's not because my bare face hurts your eyes."

She laughed and the last tears danced on her dark lashes. "Your face—bare or bearded—is like dark chocolate for my eyes." She planted a kiss on his lips. He felt it all the way to the soles of his feet.

Pulling back, she whispered, "I was hoping we could slip out early and go back to your place."

"But?" he asked.

"Tía Nona came with us tonight. I'm afraid we might have to stay a little longer than I'd hoped to take her home."

As if summoned, the old woman stepped onto the porch. "Why are you two out here? We're about to eat. Maybe you should help your cousin with the salad, *hija*, while Matthew and I get reacquainted." Tía Nona took his elbow.

Julia shot him a concerned look over the little woman's head.

"It's okay, sweetheart. I'll come find you after Nona and I catch up."

Julia lifted one eyebrow but walked into the house.

Matt looked down at the old woman. "I have a few questions for you."

Starting with asking if she knew about his father's illness. Tía Nona had been his nanny when Matt was a baby and had looked after him when he was little. One day she'd quit and never returned to Casa Larga. Matt didn't know why Nona had left, but he remembered his mother going ballistic about it.

The woman shifted her weight. "I guessed you might. Come on. Linda has set up the margarita bar in the back." She led him through a side gate to the backyard. "I haven't thought about your family in a long time and I remember better with a little tequila."

The backyard was a near perfect square with a little bit of grass and one oak tree. In the quadrant closest to the house sat an old wooden picnic table with a ragged umbrella in the middle. A small group of people had gathered around, eating chips, salsa and guacamole. They seemed to be ignoring a veggie platter and another one with cheese and crackers.

The table in the second quadrant seemed to be the bar. Matt poured the ice cubes, lime and simple sugar into a blender that was plugged into a long extension cord. There were three bottles of tequila. Nona pointed to the Jose Cuervo.

"Add a little of the Captain, too." She motioned toward the rum. "And salt the glass. I like my pirate sweet and salty."

He poured a splash of each into the blender.

"More." Tía Nona tipped the tequila bottle up,

splashing in enough to choke a donkey. Okay, then. He ran the blender and poured the slush into a salted glass in the shape of a cactus.

"¡Salud!" She lifted the glass to her lips. "Wait. You're not having any?"

He laughed. Rum and tequila? He needed a few brain cells left tonight for all the sweet and salty things he was going to do with Julia. "I'm a *cerveza* guy."

She pointed to the coolers where he found a cold bottle to his liking. Nona commandeered two lawn chairs for them and sat heavily. The chair swallowed her up. When he was a kid, he'd thought Tía Nona was bigger than life. Now she seemed tiny. How old was she, anyway? Seventy-five? Eighty?

She leaned toward him, her face stern. "I have worried about you for far too long. Tell me you turned out okay."

That kicked him back a bit. "Sure. I'm fine."

Sort of.

The image of Julia and Henry sitting with him at Juanita's popped into his head. It was like a Rockwell painting that he had no business keeping. He was alone, without a family of his own and no place to call home, but he'd be okay. He had plans for that airline he'd always wanted.

Somehow the thought didn't soothe him.

She studied him for a long beat and finally nodded. "Good."

"But I have questions."

She straightened her back. "Yes. I've waited for this day for a long time. Okay, then, ask. I am ready."

Her face might have been wrinkled and her body tired, but her eyes still snapped with the same spark as they always had. Just like Julia's. Huh. He'd never noticed that before. They did look alike, which was strange because Julia had been adopted—dropped off in Pueblicito like a puppy in a sack left on a doorstep. Nona wasn't a blood relation. He leaned closer.

Or was she?

"Tell me about Julia's mother. What happened to her?" He sipped his beer.

"What?" Her eyes widened. She clutched the salted glass like a shield against her bosom. "That's what you want to ask me? I thought you'd want to know how your mother threw me out of the house because I knew too much. Or why your father needs an angel to save his black soul."

Okay, yes. He did want to know those things, too, but Julia was more important. She always had been.

"Tell me," he said firmly.

Nona's head swung toward the house. Looking for a savior or making sure Julia was out of earshot?

She reached out and grabbed his wrist. "Julia cannot know what I am about to tell you."

"Why?"

"Because it will put her and Henry in danger, that's why." She nearly emptied the cactus glass. "I will only tell you because I know you will keep it to yourself. To keep her safe. And if Julia starts making noises like she wants to find her mother, like she does every now and again, stop her."

His heartbeat ratcheted up. "Does this have anything to do with my father?"

She opened her mouth. Closed it. Her lips were pressed together so hard that they turned white.

"Trust me, Nona. I will protect them. I need to know what the threat is."

She glanced one more time toward the kitchen. Julia was still inside. Her laughter carried across the yard like a soothing warm breeze.

"*Ojalá*, you could try to protect them. I just don't think you can."

His sense of impending danger was going off again. "I will, dammit." He had once and he would again. "I'm not a kid anymore. I will do whatever it takes to make her safe."

She chewed her lip, like Julia did when she was thinking, debating. "Julia's mother was young when she had Julia. Very young. She made mistakes and is still paying for them. What she doesn't want is for Julia to pay for them, as well."

"Julia's mother is alive?"

Julia always wondered if her parents were alive or dead. At least that was one pain she'd been spared.

"*Sí*, she is alive, but Julia must not try to find her. A deadly gang from Los Angeles is after her because she saw things. Bad things. Kidnapping, murder, drug running, this is their business. Understand? Long ago they said they'd kill her to shut her lips. They warned that they'd hurt everyone she loves."

"What the hell? So she just disappeared? Why didn't she go to the authorities?"

"She had her reasons. All of them involved keeping Julia safe." Nona was talking fast now, getting the words out in a rush. "This is my *familia*, Matthew. My loved ones. That horrible gang can't hurt my girl or sweet little Henry."

"I have to do something."

She studied him. "What would you do?"

He ran his hands through his hair. He had no answers.

"I have thought on it for years. There is nothing. Julia's mother has to keep hiding to protect them. That's the only way. You have to keep Julia out of this."

Was this the intel that RW had on Julia's family? The story he'd threatened to go public with ten years ago? What sort of a bastard would put a young girl at risk like that?

Anger pounded in Matt's chest.

"Julia's mother should've gone to the police and turned state's evidence against the gang. She should've worked with the FBI to have them all arrested. Running away from the problem? From her child? That's not acceptable."

She huffed. "One to talk."

"Excuse me?"

Nona crossed her arms, lips sealed.

Matt pushed up from his chair and paced the yard. Frustration and fury roared through him. All he could think about were those times Julia had cried on his shoulder, missing a mother who'd left her behind. Julia had grown up feeling unworthy because her parents had dumped her. He knew exactly how that felt and it pissed him off.

He turned to face Nona. "What sort of mother abandons her child?"

She puffed up in that chair like a little toad. "A mother who loves her baby more than a life of freedom. A mother who sacrificed everything—even a relationship with her child—to keep her family safe. A mother who would *never* hurt her daughter. Never beat her. What sort of mother beats her four-year-old son?"

He blinked. "What?"

He walked back and sat beside Nona.

She exhaled deeply. "You were screaming. I ran in and found her hitting you with a silver hairbrush. You had red marks all over your little arms, your sweet cheeks…" Tía Nona's eyes welled. "Your mother was a brutal woman. I fought with her. Got the brush out of her hand. She called for the guards and had me dragged out of Casa Larga. I was forbidden to return. She told everyone that I was the one who hurt you, but I swear, *mijo*. I didn't. I would never."

He looked down to see her hands holding his. Her expression was pure sorrow.

"I don't remember that," he said softly.

"It's true. Every word." She cupped his face with her hands. "Not a day went by that I didn't worry about you. I thought of you as my own, too. Just like Julia and Henry. You all are the children I couldn't have. I wanted to protect you, save you. I'm sorry I couldn't. Sometimes the world is too strong for one woman. We do what we can and that is all. Don't hate Julia's mother for her mistakes. Mine are worse. I hope you forgive me one day for not rescuing you, too."

Matt was struck silent as Nona continued to hold his hands. It was hard to process all the news he'd heard in the last couple of hours. The desire to fly a plane, any plane, tugged at him like an addiction. He needed to get into the clouds and fly away from this dysfunctional world for a while. To breathe.

"Matt! Matt!" Henry came running into the backyard, followed by a dozen kids. He stopped short in front of them. His eyebrows shot up like he'd never seen anything quite so strange as Tía Nona holding a man's hands before.

"Come on. Anthony's mom bought a huge piñata that looks like SpongeBob. It's about to pop with all the candy stuffed inside."

Matt had seen a piñata at a birthday party before. Blindfolded kids took turns swinging a bat at a papier-mâché creature until they busted it to bits and all the candy came flying out. To make the game more difficult, adults pulled the piñata up and away when the bat came close.

Matt patted Nona's hand and gently pulled his free. "What do you need me to do? Pull the rope?"

"No, Anthony's brother has that covered. We want you to swing the bat with us. Maybe after me, so that I get one good shot."

"Really? Isn't that for you kids? I don't want to take someone's turn."

Henry took his arm and pulled. "Pleeeease? I want you to. The guys all say it's okay."

No kid had ever looked at him with such adoring eyes before. It made Matt's heart swell with an emotion he couldn't identify. "All right, then. Let's go annihilate SpongeBob."

To Tía Nona he said, "Thanks for everything, *tía*. I mean it. You raised Julia in a loving home. There's nothing to forgive."

He hadn't asked if she believed RW truly had a mental illness. Part of him already knew the answer.

Sixteen

Julia watched them through the living room window.

Matt had asked her to be the keeper of his cell phone and car keys while he "taught SpongeBob a lesson or two." He lined up as if he was on a baseball diamond, moving his hips and loosening his shoulders. Man, he was cute. She snapped a picture of him with his cell phone. He took one giant swing and the piñata was toast. Poor SpongeBob's head went flying off and the rest was broken into ragged pieces. With Matt's final hit, candy shot out and rained sweet hail all over the backyard. The kids scrambled to grab it all up. She took another picture.

"Oh, no, you don't! That's mine." Matt lifted his blindfold and dove into the grass with them. It was a mass frenzy of arms and legs as they all fought for the loot. The laughter and squeals permeated the yard and came through the open windows.

"Hope he's okay," Julia said to herself. And snapped more pictures.

"Oh, that man is way past okay. He is *divine*," Tía Flora said behind her.

Julia turned to see her three aunts and her cousin Linda all peeking out the window at her boyfriend.

Um. Boyfriend? Was that what he was?

Her boyfriend for the weekend.

"He's a very good boy," Tía Nona said.

All during Julia's growing-up years, Nona had tried to keep her from seeing Matt, always warning Julia about dangerous pirates, and now he was a *very* good boy? What had Matt put in Tía Nona's drink?

"I should know, I raised him myself." Tía Nona nodded.

"You did what, now?" Julia faced her aunt.

"Didn't I tell you?" Nona waved her hand as if this revelation was no big deal. "I was his nanny a long time ago. Bottle-fed him myself."

"No, you never told me," Julia said. "Why didn't you—?"

Tía Alana interrupted. "¡*Cuidado!* Hope those boys don't squish his manhood with that wrestling."

Linda shook her head. "Mother! Only Julia can talk about his manhood."

"Right, right. Sorry, Julia. It's just not that often I have such a good-looking man right there in the backyard."

"Um, it's okay." But she, too, hoped the boys didn't squish his manhood. She had plans for him later.

Matt flipped over and shielded Henry from the other wrestlers. When had Henry laughed that hard before? She couldn't remember.

Linda gripped her elbow. "That's daddy material right there."

If only Henry's daddy would decide to stay.

"Uncle! Uncle! You win. The candy is all yours. Get off me, you bandits." Laughing, Matt lifted the last kid off his shoulder. "Go. Eat it all."

They scrambled away, high-fiving each other for taking down the man.

He hadn't had this much fun since…huh. He couldn't remember. Did these rascals know how good they had it? They got to be real kids.

He dusted off his pants. He had grass stains everywhere. And he bent to rub some of the dirt off his shoes. So much for trying to make a good impression.

"Having fun?" Julia stood over him.

He grinned. "Best party I've been to in forever."

"Better than RW's pirate party last night?" There was a whole lot of heat in her eyes. It charged him up.

"The dancing was the best part of that one but…" He shrugged. "This one has candy."

She laughed. "You really do like sweets, don't you?"

"Oh, babe, you have no idea. I have a bad craving." He stepped close and tipped her chin up.

Her lids were hooded. "Are you hungry now?"

"Starved." By the blush on her cheeks, she knew what he meant. "After we take Tía Nona home, we're going back to my place. I have a promise to keep. Four times in a row. I'd like you to think on that for a while." No use in him being the only one hot and bothered.

She shivered in a good way. "Promises, promises."

"I keep them."

They passed the group of folks eating chips and

salsa and drinking margaritas. Julia walked beside him, her arm casually hooked with his as if they went to family barbecues like this every weekend.

Was this what it was to be at peace? Happy?

They walked over to Maria and her boyfriend. Jaime was grilling steaks and roasting some evil-looking peppers. The smoke was loaded with flavor and Matt's stomach growled.

When she saw Matt, Maria tipped her chin in a tough-girl maneuver. "Looks like the eye is healing."

"Yep. Didn't feel a thing." He ignored her and focused on the food. "Looks good."

"Here, man. Try this." Jaime sliced off two chunks of steak and dipped it in homemade salsa. He gave one mouthful to Matt on a toothpick and ate the other himself.

"Mmm. That's good." Matt chewed. "Spicy." His eyes started to water almost as badly as when Maria had punched him.

"That's my special volcano salsa. Like it?" Jaime acted like his mouth wasn't burning like lava.

The heat growing in Matt's mouth was blowing out his sinuses. His ears were tingling. He didn't dare spit it out or Jaime would think he was a total wimp. But if he swallowed, it might burn a hole in his intestines.

"Yeah," Matt croaked. "Water."

Julia hustled over and grabbed him a water bottle. He downed half of it in one gulp.

Julia was concerned. "Too hot for you?"

"I might have burned my tongue off."

"On no, that is a real shame. Right, Julia?" Maria said.

Julia gave her the side-eye.

"Steaks are ready, baby, just the way you like them. Thick and juicy." Jaime swatted Maria's butt.

Julia was watching their exchange.

"Is that the way you like your…meat? Spicy?" Matt whispered in her ear.

She gulped. "Yes?"

"Question marks, babe. They're your tell." He kissed her temple. "I know what you like."

"Really? Is this on the menu?" In one of the biggest surprises in a day chock-full of them, she swatted his behind.

He had no words. In a crowded backyard, full of her relatives and easily a third of the town, she kissed him. It was one of the highlights of the day. He couldn't wait for more.

The rest of the night was filled with laughter, good food and good-natured grilling. Matt and Julia sat with the adults while Henry went to the kids' table. When Julia's family started asking questions about their plans, Matt suddenly wished he could sit with the kids. Man, Julia's relatives were relentless.

Julia tried deflection and subject-changing, and when those stopped working, she raised her hands in defeat. He ended the line of questioning with, "You know, folks, we just found each other again. Please give us a chance to work through everything in private."

They finished eating and people carried their plates to the kitchen to be washed. Matt was busy watching Julia bend over to put the plates in the dishwasher when Henry came up behind Matt and yanked on his shirt. "Is it true?"

"What's that?"

Henry's eyes were wide. He had a goofy grin on his face. "Are you going to be my dad?"

All the family's talk about the future…they'd led to this. And the emotions. He couldn't even begin to sort them out. It was like a rogue tidal wave that came roaring out of a glassy sea. His heart was utterly and completely swamped. With regret that Henry wasn't his. With longing, for what it would be like if Henry was his son. With heartbreak because he didn't know how to be a father, or how to create a future with Julia that would allow Henry to remain in his life.

And because Matt didn't know what to say, he spoke the truth. "That would be an honor, Henry. Any man would be lucky to be a dad to a great guy like you."

For the third time that day, he was bro-hugged. Only this time it wasn't a surprise because Matt started it.

Julia turned around to see them. "What's this all about?"

They released each other.

"Nothing," Henry said.

Matt didn't lie to Julia. Never had, never would. It wasn't like he could speak with the lump in his throat, anyway, so he said nothing at all.

"One more time for the camera," she said, lifting his cell phone. He'd forgotten he'd given it to her for safekeeping.

Matt put his arm around Henry and they smiled for the picture.

Seventeen

It was after ten when Julia drove Tía Nona home and Matt followed behind her in the Lamborghini. Henry rode shotgun in his car. The kid was so tired that he fell asleep on the leather seat and was snoring two minutes after they'd left the party.

Matt didn't mind. He drove nice and easy and kept the sound system off. He idled the sports car outside Tía Nona's house and waited for Julia.

Tía Nona herself toddled over to his side of the car to speak to him.

He put his window down. "Good night, *tía*. It was nice hanging out with you."

"Buenas noches, mijo." She leaned in and put her hand on his shoulder. "Don't be a stranger. Come see me before you leave town. I have something for you."

He frowned. "What is it?"

She shook her finger at him. "Visit me tomorrow and find out."

When they got to Julia's house, he carried the dead-to-the-world kid to his bed. Julia removed Henry's shoes and socks and tucked him under the covers.

"He's amazing, Julia. So damned cute," Matt said softly.

"They all are when they're asleep."

"Can I?" He took out his cell phone for a picture.

"He won't mind if you take his picture. He's pretty ga-ga over you, in case you didn't know." There was a rap on the front door. "It's my neighbor. She's going to babysit for a few hours while we go to your place. But I need to be back by midnight, okay?"

"Sure."

He took the picture while Julia gave her babysitter final instructions. Matt had never been conflicted about sleeping with a woman before, but for some inexplicable reason, he wasn't racing out the door and dragging Julia with him. Part of him wanted to stay right here, in Julia's comfortable, beautiful, love-filled home, with her and Henry.

He knew she didn't want him to sleep over, he got that. She was the mom and he respected her wishes.

But he couldn't help thinking about how cool it would be to see Julia first thing in the morning and wake her with kisses down her back. And he'd never had a kid jump on the bed or want to climb in when monsters scared him. He'd never slept night after night with a woman, either.

Damn, he wanted—no, a better word was *craved*—things he couldn't have. Might never have.

You've got tonight, man. Don't ruin it.

He kissed Henry's forehead, tucked the blankets in tighter and followed Julia out.

They held hands and walked through the gardens to the pool house. It was scary how comfortable she felt strolling the Harper grounds. With Matt, everything felt good.

She wouldn't let herself think about the flip side of that coin because she only had about twenty-four hours before he flew away.

He opened the door and turned on the lights.

"We're back," Julia said softly. Why did she feel like she had to whisper?

He pulled her into his arms. "Finally."

"Did you have fun tonight?"

"I did. I enjoy hanging out with your family. Because they love you and aren't afraid to show it."

She put her head on his chest. The pounding in her ear was strong. "I know."

"Julia?"

"Hmm?" She looked up. His expression was serious.

"You're surrounded by so much love… Do you still want to know what happened to your mom?"

She frowned. "Yes, of course."

He exhaled slowly. "What if knowing could put your family in danger? Would you still want to know?"

She stepped back. "What's this about, Matt?"

"Seems your mom got mixed up with a tough crowd before she had you. She left you with Tía Nona to keep you safe. That's about all I know. But I have a source I can talk to. Maybe I can get you closure on this. Do you want me to try?"

She hadn't imagined that she'd ever know what really happened with her mother. And of all the scenarios she'd imagined over the years, her mother involved with bad guys wasn't one of them.

"Yes," she said quietly. "As long as you're discreet and stay safe. I don't want to put anyone in danger. If it looks like someone could get hurt, leave it. I have lived this long without a mother." She sighed. "But it would be nice to know. Thank you."

"Okay. I'll see what I can find out for you." He pulled her back to him. Then he cupped her jaw and kissed her. Softly at first, gentle. It was good, but she wanted more. She reached around and grabbed his butt, angling into him.

He scooped her up in his arms and carried her to his bed.

Her heart was already pounding like crazy. She crooked her finger at him so he would come closer and then she unbuttoned his shirt. "Since this afternoon, I have been dying to get my hands on you."

"Are you sure you weren't after my candy?" His blue eyes sparkled.

Was that a euphemism?

He pulled a Mexican candy out of his shirt pocket. "I had to hide it from those kids. They stole the rest of my piñata loot, but I love this kind. Juanita makes them."

She laughed out loud. "You do love your sweets."

His eyebrow lifted. "And my spicy." He pressed her back into the bed and kissed the daylights out of her.

Pushing the shirt off his shoulders, she ran her hands over his chest. He was so beautiful. Every curve, every muscle, felt like coming home. Pulling her lips away, she said, "Strip, Captain. We don't have much time tonight."

He grinned and, jumping up beside her on the bed, stretched out. Next to her. Naked.

He was gorgeous.

She was rusty, and inexperienced. Probably not like any of the women he'd had sex with. But she didn't want to think about that. She cleared her throat and ran her finger down his chest. "What would you like me to do?"

He touched her hip. "Everything you do works for me."

She looked down. Yep. Her simple touch was working. It empowered her. She flattened her hands on his belly and rubbed across his abs. How did he get so fit?

She touched his back, feeling the muscles quiver under her fingers. She massaged his buttocks, enjoying the bunching of muscle in her hand. Coming back around his hip bone, she circled his belly button and played with the dark hairs below it. His breath was coming faster.

She bit her lip and looked into his eyes. Wow. It hit her so hard.

This beautiful man was her Matt.

Alive. Amazing.

She took his penis in her hands and watched him suck in a sharp breath. Their eyes remained locked as she began to rub him. When she ran her thumb across his silky head, he groaned. "Oh, sweetheart. Like that."

He kissed her, sucking her bottom lip.

She almost came right then.

"I can't wait any longer. Take off your clothes." His voice was husky. He reached into his dresser and pulled out a condom. When she was naked, too, and he was ready, he kissed her neck, sending shivers everywhere.

"Top or bottom?" he asked.

"Huh? Oh. Top."

"Your wish is my command." He smiled and flipped her over on top of him. "Hell, Julia, you're so beautiful it hurts. Sit up so I can look at you."

She straddled him.

Pure adoration. That's what she saw in his expression. Easing him inside her, she began a slow, intense ride. Deep in, slow drag out.

He let out a short breath. "You feel so good."

Her reservations, insecurities and sense of smallness went away.

He held her hips, keeping her pressed down. Their eyes were still locked. She could see emotions swirling in his widened pupils. His grip was getting harder, his breath faster. She was getting close, too. She picked up the pace. Faster, deeper.

"Oh, babe," he said in a way that made her melt.

He rose and cupped her breast like a treasure in his hand. He kissed the underside and then took her nipple in his warm mouth. He sucked and rolling waves of ecstasy took over. She closed her eyes and continued to rock, shooting up and over the edge. One time. Two times. The pleasure was overwhelming. Her cadence slowed. She was losing steam.

He flipped her again and took over. The pace was intense. The bed pounded into the backboard. And... oh, she was coming again. She cried out.

He collapsed on top of her. After a couple of minutes he eased off to the side so that he wouldn't be too heavy, but stayed joined with her. Perfect. Good feelings were still humming through her core.

He rubbed her arms and down her sides, as if trying to touch her everywhere all at once. She could still feel him inside, pressing her sensitive spots.

"Matt, oh, oh." And just like that, without any movement, she came again.

Four times. Just like he promised.

That was the last thing she thought before she fell asleep.

Somewhere she could hear singing and recognized the song about a pirate turning forty. Matt was rubbing her cheek and she felt so good.

Don't stop. Don't ever—

She opened her eyes. "Henry! What time is it?"

"It's okay, I set my alarm. It's eleven thirty. We'd better get dressed and get going." He kissed her gently before he rolled over and turned the alarm off. The pirate song stopped. "You are so sexy when you snore. I might've taken a hundred pictures while you slept."

"You did not." She shoved him lightly.

He grinned. "You're right. I did not. But I wanted to so bad."

What was his obsession with taking pictures of her and Henry?

Once they were dressed, he took her hand in his and didn't let go until they were back at the car. They didn't say much. He was strangely quiet.

When he pulled into her driveway and stopped the car he said, "I'll walk you up."

"No need. I'll just tiptoe in and let the babysitter out."

He took her hand in his as if he wasn't going to let her go. "I'll be here bright and early. I've got plans for us. Big plans. Tell Henry he'd better find a superhero T-shirt."

"That will make him destroy the rest of his room. What should I wear?"

"Is nothing on the table?"

She shook her head.

"Dammit. Okay, then jeans and walking shoes. Maybe bring a sweater." He checked his watch. "Twelve oh one. You'd better go in."

It was his last day in Plunder Cove already. She leaned over and kissed him quickly and hustled out of the car before her tears ruined everything.

Eighteen

The sun hadn't officially come up yet, but Matt couldn't wait. He stood at Julia's darkened door and knocked. He heard movement inside.

"Sweetheart. It's me."

"What time is it? I'm not dressed."

"Good."

She opened up slowly. Her hair was messed. Her makeup was gone. She was wearing a gray tank top that did little to hide her precious curves and a pair of pink silk shorts that perfectly adorned her bare legs.

He lifted a bouquet of wildflowers, twice as big as the ones he'd brought yesterday. "Go ahead. Smash the hell out of them."

Her grin spread. She grabbed him by the collar and gave him a yank. They crashed into the same wall—lip to lip, pounding heart to heart, body to body.

When she released him to catch a breath she said, "Good morning."

"I think we've found our sunrise ritual."

She sighed. "Today's our last day together."

They locked eyes.

He tried to dive in deep so that he'd never have to come back out. He cupped her cheek and kissed her lips softly. "Then we'd better love the hell out of it."

"Coffee?" Her voice cracked.

"Please." He sat at the kitchenette and watched her get the coffee going. Then he pulled her into his lap. "Missed you last night. I wish you didn't have to leave."

She leaned her head back on his shoulder. "Missed you, too. But I couldn't leave Henry alone."

"I get it—"

"What time is it?" Henry came into the kitchen in his pajamas. He was rubbing his eyes.

"Half past the butt-crack of dawn," Matt said.

Henry snorted. "You said 'butt-crack.'"

Julia stood. "Oh, boy. It's going to be one of *those* days." Her voice sounded mom-ish. Hell, he loved it. He couldn't get enough of all the amazing sides of Julia.

"It sure is. Get yourself ready, Henry. We've got a great adventure planned. Think Superman," Matt said.

"What? Oh, no way! Are we going to fly?" The kid's face split open with happiness.

Matt grinned. "Maybe."

"Yippee!" Henry punched the air. "What plane are we going in? Mr. Harper's new one?"

Matt shrugged. "I'll have to see which one is available for us. Go get ready, brush your teeth, scratch your butt—you know, whatever you kids do."

Henry was halfway out of the kitchen before he turned around. "Like this?" He scratched his backside.

"Yep." Matt scratched his, too.

Julia rolled her eyes. "Oh, wow. Could there be any more boy humor in this kitchen?"

Matt laughed. He was enjoying this little family moment way too much. "You'd better get a move on, too. I'm hungry and breakfast is calling." And then acted like he was going to swat her butt, too, but his hand lingered instead.

She turned and gave him a smokin' hot look. "You trying to get something started, Matt Harper?"

"Maybe." Hell, with that look, he already had. File that intel away for further inspection.

When Henry and Julia left the kitchen, Matt felt a sudden loss, like a hole opened up in the universe and sucked all the good stuff out. He sat down at the tiny kitchenette table. Glancing around the small kitchen with the crammed appliances and far too few cabinets, he realized he felt more comfortable here than anywhere else. The knowledge hurt.

Here didn't belong to him. He had to leave it and all the good stuff behind.

An hour later they were flying over the ocean. Henry was in the back seat trying to see everything out the windows while playing with the headset. Julia was in the copilot seat, quietly taking everything in.

Matt settled into his captain's seat, enjoying every damned second. God, he loved flying. It had only been two days on the ground but he'd missed jetting through the sky. The feeling of lifting off and leaving his troubles behind was addictive. He didn't want to think about what it meant that he'd been so eager to share this with Julia and Henry.

It was a great day to fly. The Pacific Ocean was a sparkling navy blue with swaths of turquoise. The sky was streaked with orange and yellow as the sun came up. Winds were almost nonexistent. Perfect. He did one lazy circle over Plunder Cove.

"Look down, Henry. That's Casa Larga. Wave at Old Man Harper."

Henry waved. "I don't see him."

"That's because he's stuck on his throne or locking people in the dungeon."

"Matt! He's kidding, Henry," Julia said through his headset.

Less than a minute later Henry asked, "Where are we going?"

"Santa Barbara. Should take us about half an hour. Keep your eyes on the coast and soon you'll see the purple-blue mountains. That's when you will know we are almost there."

"What's in Santa Barbara?" Henry asked.

"Breakfast," Matt said, rubbing his stomach.

"Can we fly over my house first?" Henry asked.

"Sure thing." Matt performed a large eight in the sky and came back around.

"You love this, don't you?" Julia said softly. He couldn't read her expression. It seemed like an odd swirl of sadness and admiration.

"Flying? Hell, yes. It's what I was born to do. The only thing I'm good at."

"I'd say there are other things you are good at doing." Her cheeks were pink.

"Sweetheart, after breakfast I'll try to beat my score."

She bit her lip. "Yes, please."

"There it is!" Henry yelled. "Wow. Pueblicito looks so small."

"It's not the size that matters." Matt winked at Julia.

"Can you do some tricks?"

"Tricks?"

"Yeah spirals, rolls, dives, something." Henry bounced on his seat.

Julia shook her head. "No! There will be no crazy tricks."

"I have to agree with your mom. RW probably wouldn't love you getting sick on his plane."

"Fine." Henry crossed his arms. "But you know how to do wicked maneuvers, right? Like in war and stuff. If bad guys were shooting at the plane."

Where was the kid going with this line of questioning?

"If there was shooting, I'd pull out the stops to keep you two safe. The Air Force trained me to outfox the bad guys. Luckily, we don't have to worry about that this morning."

Henry was quiet for a moment and then he said, "Guess my dad didn't do it right—the fox thing—'cuz they shot him down."

Julia made a strange garbled sound. Her face went pale and the look in her eyes was panicky. Her hands were in tight fists. Just the mention of the guy knocked her on her ass. Her reaction made something in his chest burn.

"I'm really sorry about that. Search and rescue was the part of my job I loved the most. Saving lives is the biggest rush. I wish I could've found him for you guys." He also wished he could pull Julia into his lap and kiss the sadness out of her lips. Kiss her until she couldn't remember any other man but him. "Sorry to bring up bad memories. That was insensitive of me."

"No, it's not you. I just… Henry doesn't…and you don't…" She swirled her hand in the air as if to link the words together in a way that made sense.

The only thing clear was that she still loved Henry's father. And Matt was never going to change that.

Right. He needed to stick with the plan. One last sexy weekend and then he would bug out and build that airline he'd always wanted.

Throwing out the game plan wasn't an option.

A half hour later Matt touched down at the private airport in Santa Barbara. It was a small Spanish building with palm trees around the front.

"Perfect landing," Julia said.

He cocked an eyebrow. "It could've been smoother."

She'd never experienced such a graceful landing. Matt was an impressive pilot. In the pilot's seat, he was both relaxed and energized. Comfortable and alert. He flew the skies the way he rode his bikes—one with the machine. Flying seemed to pull together his broken pieces and connect him with the wind, the clouds, that endless blue sky. She'd never seen him in his true element before today and it tore her up. He didn't belong in Plunder Cove. Grounding him would rob him of the freedom he craved and the life he'd longed to have since she could remember. How could she do that to him?

She wouldn't do that to him.

"You okay? You've been a little quiet." Matt studied her.

"I'm fine." But he wasn't imagining things. She hadn't said much since Henry had brought up his dad. With her fumbling reaction, he must've thought she'd lost her mind, and he'd be right. She'd almost blurted out that he was Henry's father right then.

She'd started to think she should tell him the truth. But when? And how? The longer he believed that Henry's father was shot down in Afghanistan, the harder it would be.

Would he feel trapped? Would he think he had to give up his dreams? Would he love their son?

Would he still leave Plunder Cove?

Her heart hurt.

"Are we getting out now?" Henry interrupted her thoughts.

"Yep," Matt said to Henry but his intense gaze was still on her face. "Ready?"

No. She had no idea what she was going to do. But to him she said, "Absolutely. Let's go."

Nineteen

Back at Plunder Cove, Angel's cell phone rang. It startled her because she didn't get many calls and it took her three rings to find the darned thing. The screen read No Caller ID. Her heart pounded. Only one person outside Plunder Cove had Angel's number and she was instructed to call only in emergencies. It was too dangerous otherwise.

"Cristina?"

"Yeah, Angel, it's me. I have to talk fast."

"Are you in trouble?"

"Not me. I'm freaking out about you."

Angel sat heavily. "Tell me."

"A dude was poking around, asking questions. Says he's helping you. Says he's looking for info on Cuchillo, like he knows you two were a couple. Like he's a cop! That's a freaking bad idea, *mujer*." Cristina's voice was a low growl. "Cuchillo likes using his knives, especially on snitches, you know that."

She did. And she knew a lot of other things that kept her awake at night. "I haven't talked to the cops. I promised you I wouldn't. I'm not putting your son or my family in danger."

"Someone talked."

Why would anyone be asking about her after all these years? Unless…oh, no. "The guy." She pressed the ache in her forehead as understanding bored into her brain. "Was he a private investigator?"

"Said he was, but smelled like cop."

RW! He must have hired someone to investigate the gang. This is what happened when she spilled her darkest secrets. She'd found some sort of solace at the time, but now she felt sick. The world started to spin. "I'll call the man off."

"It's too late. I told him I'd tell him if the gang was getting close to finding you. But now…" There was a beat of silence. Angel could picture the girl…well, really a woman now, checking to make sure no one was listening. The gang had ears everywhere. "I think they saw me talking to the dude, or something, because everyone's…I dunno…weird around me. They're stirred up but won't tell me why."

So, she was in trouble.

"Listen, Cristina, don't take any chances. Take your little boy and get out. Come here. It's safe and quiet."

"Nuh-uh. You're not hearing me, Angel. I said it's too late."

The tone in Cristina's voice rang layer after layer of danger bells in her body. *If they find me…*

"Why?" she whispered.

"That cop dude is dead."

Ohgodohgodohgod. The floor dropped out beneath her feet. She knew. Cristina didn't have to tell her that the gang had tortured the man for information before killing him.

Now they knew about her.

They were coming.

RW knocked on Angel's door. He had flowers and a bottle of wine. She didn't answer. He heard a noise around the back of her house and followed the sound.

Angel was in the shed. He took a few seconds to watch her reach up to get something on the top shelf. He loved her womanly curves.

"Can I help?" he asked.

She screamed and spun around, holding the gardening hoe like a weapon.

"RW! You scared me."

"I can see that. Safe to approach?"

She put the hoe down. "Sorry. Yes."

But he didn't see the glorious smile he was used to, or the light in her eyes. In fact, she had worried wrinkles around her mouth. He dipped his head and kissed each line.

She sighed. Wrapping her arms around his neck, she pressed her lips to his and kissed him deeply. It was an amazing kiss that both charged him up and scared the hell out of him. Something was wrong.

After a while he pulled back and looked into her beautiful face. Fear. Right there sparking in the edges of her brown eyes and in the tightness to her mouth. And now that his eyes had fully adjusted to the dim light in the shed, he saw boxes behind her.

"Packing?" he asked, terrified of the answer.

"We need to talk." She took his hand and led him out of the shed and into her home. "Want something to drink?"

"Am I going to need it?" he joked, trying to play it casual, light. Even while his insides churned.

Her smile flickered and went dim. "Maybe." She opened the wine he'd brought and poured it into her glass and poured sparkling water into his. They clinked.

She sat on the arm of the couch. Close, so close. Never close enough.

He put his glass down on the table and rubbed her arm. "What's going on?"

"Did you…?" He could hear her swallow hard, like her throat was tight. She took a sip of wine and tried again. "Did you hire a private investigator to go to Los Angeles and dig up my past?"

How did she find out? That jackass was supposed to be discreet. "I was trying to get information to protect you, Angel. Don't you want to stop running?"

She leaned into him. "Yes. I'd give everything I have to settle here for good, with you. Everything but my family."

Okay. He liked all of that except the agony in her voice.

"These past years with you, RW, have been…" She started to cry. "You have given me so much that I don't deserve."

He took the glass from her hand and pulled her into his lap, cradling her head on his chest. "That's where you are wrong, my angel. You've given me life. You've changed me. It's far more than a man like me could ever hope for. Tell me what's wrong."

"The PI you sent to Los Angeles. They killed him."

"No." He slammed his eyes shut and exhaled through his teeth. "Those bastards!"

"Because of me…another man is dead." She was sobbing, her body heaving.

He tipped her face up so he could kiss her tears away. God, the sorrow on her face ripped through him like a serrated knife. "My fault, not yours. We'll make them pay, Angel. They are not getting away with this."

"No. Don't you see? I can't risk you or other people I love getting hurt because of my mistakes. Cuchillo is my problem, not yours. The gang was my gang before I knew what they were capable of. I ran to save my family. This is on me!"

"How is it your mistake? You were a child living on the streets when the gang found you. Hell, thirteen, scared and alone? I probably would've joined a gang, too. They welcomed you in and protected you as if they were your family. No shame in that. You didn't break the law. You didn't kill anyone. Cuchillo took advantage of your plight and your big heart. He stole your innocence and made you witness horrible things so that you wouldn't run. It took guts to get away. That bastard deserves to be locked up forever."

Her chin still quivered. "But I can't stop him. No one can."

"I can. I have contacts, money, power. He's never come across a guy like me before. Let me fix this."

She pressed her hand to her mouth. Thinking.

He took her other hand and kissed her palm. "Please. I need you, Angel. I want to marry you. I want us to live happily with our kids and grandkids all around. Let me be your knight in shining armor this time."

"I don't want to put your family in danger, too."

"I've set up guards all around, by land and sea. We won't let them get anywhere near Plunder Cove. I promise."

She let out a deep exhale. "I'm sorry, RW. I know you mean well, but I can't have anyone else hurt because of me. If I hear they are coming, I will leave Plunder Cove. To save us all."

Twenty

They rented a car and ate at a quaint restaurant on the breakwater in Santa Barbara.

"What's this breakfast called again?" Henry asked with a full mouth.

"Belgian waffle á la mode," Matt said. "Do you like it?"

"Ice cream for breakfast? Big, big love," Henry said, shoveling in another bite.

Julia pressed close to him, smiling. He felt the heat against him and touched her hand with his. He wanted her, always. He loved this day already and it had barely begun. Happy was a foreign concept he could get used to.

"What does tying a knot have to do with marriage?" Henry asked. Julia turned stone-cold still. Her face drained of color just like it had in the plane when Henry had asked questions about his dad.

"Oh, Henry, we're not—" she began.

Matt rushed ahead of her. "Some guys would say the knot goes around your neck like a tie." He imitated pulling a tie tight, complete with crossing his eyes and sticking his tongue out. Henry laughed. Julia sat in silence.

"I'm not one of those guys." He looked at Julia's ashen face and took her hand in his. "You see, a rope is strong. Really strong, right? But tie a tight knot in it and a miracle happens. When individual strands are bound together like this…" He held up their joined hands. "Everything is stronger. Better. Unstoppable. That's why I asked your mom to marry me a long time ago. I believed that with her I could conquer the world." He met her eyes. Would she see the depth of his feelings?

One tear rolled down her cheek. Why? What was she thinking? Was he strong enough to hear her sweet lips admit she'd only loved one man—Henry's father?

Hell, no.

Because he was scared, he rushed on. "But marriage isn't for everyone." He shrugged. "I don't feel bad about that and neither should you. Life is short. Let's enjoy what we have."

She let out a breath as if she'd been holding it the whole time he'd been speaking. "Thank you."

"For what?"

"Loving me back then. For this last weekend."

He kissed her hand, not ready to confront how much

he was feeling right now, not just back then. "Who's ready for a surrey ride along the beachfront?"

"Me!" Henry cheered. "What's a surrey? Do I get to drive?"

Twenty-One

After they landed back in Plunder Cove, they all piled into her ugly old car. The lime-green Nissan Cube looked pathetic parked in RW's private parking lot next to his sleek and expensive planes. It was another reminder of how different her life was from Matt's.

When she was young she'd hardly noticed how poor her family was and Matt hadn't seemed to care. He'd treated her like she was special. Treasured. It was incredible, really, how easily he'd slipped into her lifestyle when his family was so wealthy. It could give a person whiplash jetting to California's Riviera for breakfast one moment and put-putting in her junky car the next.

She forced her insecure thoughts out of her mind. Driving to Pueblicito, she turned down the first street and continued until the road ran out. She parked in the dirt and took her binoculars out of the trunk. There was a fog bank sitting on the horizon. The ocean breeze danced in her hair, cooling her skin.

"Follow my lead. I know how to spot the nests, but we won't get close enough to step on them, I promise."

"Hell, do you know how sexy you are right now? You sound like a cross between a zoologist and a sheriff."

She smiled. "Which do you prefer?"

"You," he whispered in her ear. "Any way I can get you." Her heart cracked. They were down to hours now.

They crossed the dirt and walked in the tall grass at the broken edge of the street, stopping at a flimsy sign tilting in the grass. "A year ago, I pounded half a dozen signs here, advising how to protect the endangered snowy plovers."

She didn't have any right to stop people from walking on the grass or the sand, but she'd hoped her signs reminded beachgoers to be careful. Until she had legal clout, it was the best she could do.

She went on. "RW had his men take them down and sent me a cease and desist order. Your family has always let people walk across 'Harper' grass to get to the beach, but putting up signs in this area is not allowed."

"What did you do?"

"I put up more. And down they went. This is the last sign I have until I can scrounge up money to have more made." She shook her head. "My last purchase of schoolbooks wiped out my savings."

"Count me in. Where do I contribute to the sign project?" He rubbed her shoulder. It was a touch of kindness, an act of solidarity, and it turned her on.

How did he do that? No one else had ever made her feel important and sexy all at once.

"Mom, can I hold the binoculars?" Henry asked.

"Sure." She lifted the strap off her neck. Her hands were a little wobbly, which might have to do with how closely Matt was standing to her and how good he smelled, and because he was the only person other than Henry who had wanted to come out here to learn about the birds. Her friends and family thought she was nuts. Everyone else hated her for wanting to restrict the beach.

"This is a good place to stop. Talk softly, we don't want to scare the mother birds," she said.

Henry searched the sand with the binoculars. "Is that one?"

She squinted. "No. Look. See that bird? Pale gray-brown with a white chest? That's a snowy plover."

Matt wore his aviator glasses and turned his head toward her pointed finger. "I see it. Damn, it is small."

She nodded. "Each one weighs up to two ounces. They get to be about six inches long. There's about two thousand snowy plovers left along the Pacific coast since most of their nesting habitat has been destroyed by development. Twenty-eight major nesting sites remain. When walkers, ATV users, horseback riders and dogs go on the beach during the breeding season, eggs and chicks are inadvertently killed. That's why they're in trouble. The species is dying out before our very eyes, and no one…" Her voice was choked with conviction and frustration. "No one will help me."

Before she knew what was happening he turned her around and kissed her. She melted into his embrace and took refuge in his warm, strong arms and soothing lips.

And, for that moment, she wasn't fighting everything by herself. She wasn't scared and battling uphill. She wasn't guarding her heart against the time when he would say goodbye.

It was Matt and Julia against the world again. God, she needed him.

Rubbing her cheek with the pad of his thumb, he said softly, "Hey, you aren't alone. You know that, right?"

No, she was worse than alone. She was happy, but fully aware it was a temporary state. He woke her from darkness with his heat and light. Tomorrow his warmth would be gone and she'd be just like the Pacific snowy plover on the brink of extinction. How would she survive losing him again?

"I see a nest," Henry soft-yelled.

"Where?" Matt released her and took his body heat with him. The cold settled quickly into her bones.

She took a deep breath to calm herself. "Can I see the binoculars for a moment, Henry?"

"Over there by that little clump of grass. Eggs, right?"

She followed his instructions and… "Good job. Yes. That's a nest. Here, Matt, you look."

He took the binoculars from her and focused. "I don't…wait…okay, yes, I see small eggs." Matt scanned the beach with the binoculars and stopped suddenly. He pulled the glass away from his eyes and looked again. Focused.

She saw the way he ground his molars together. "What is it?"

"Tractor tracks near the hatchery area." Anger rippled across his handsome features. "RW was here."

He brought the binoculars up and searched the ocean. "Two boats. See them at eleven o'clock?"

Julia looked into the water. "Eleven…? Oh, yes. I do. Who are they?"

"Dad's goons."

"What're they doing out there?" Henry asked.

Matt's voice was tight. "I can make a guess. They want to block our attempts to stop the development project. They see us. They'll be calling in the troops. Well, guess what? We attack first."

She didn't like the sound of that.

Henry's eyes sparkled. "Hooah! Let's get them."

Julia held up her hand. "Whatever happens, you need to stay out of it, Henry."

Matt took his cell phone out of his pocket. "I'm calling my brother. Maybe we can crash RW's meeting with his contractor." He dialed. "Yeah, it's me. I'm out here near the beach. When's the contractor meeting?… Good. We'll be there."

"Okay, team." Matt kissed her on the forehead and messed up Henry's hair. "Back to the Batmobile. We've got a species to save."

Jeff met them at the front entry to Casa Larga. "The gang's all here."

Matt felt Julia's nervous energy. They didn't know how this would play out. Maybe they should've left Henry at home.

But Matt had wanted to give her this win before their time was up. And he hadn't wanted to miss the chance to catch RW in the act.

"They're in the great hall. What's the game plan?" Jeff asked.

"Obstruction," Matt replied. "We won't let him do this."

Jeff shrugged. "Okay. Let's go."

They strode into the great hall as if they owned the place. RW was standing over several plans spread out across the dining table. A white-haired man stood beside him, and two younger associates hung back in case they were called to action.

RW looked up. "What's this about?"

Matt stepped forward. He could see a rather large building on the plans. "Your secret plans. Did you think we wouldn't figure it out?"

Color drained from RW's face. "How? Who told you?"

Matt was pissed now. "We have eyes! Did you think we're that stupid?"

"Leave us," RW said to the contracting team.

The three men quickly left the room and closed the doors behind them.

"You must swear you won't tell anyone," RW said softly. "Angel could be in terrible danger if anyone finds out she is here. They'll kill her."

The expression about the pin dropping in a quiet room? Yeah, that was nothing compared to the sucking silence in the great hall.

"Swear to me." RW wasn't angry. No, Matt saw desperation in his eyes. Angel was the lady who had nursed him back to health, right? Was that why RW had his goons stationed in the boats offshore? As lookouts?

What did this have to do with the snowy plovers?

"We're here about the secret development on the beach. What's it going to be? A snack shop? Jet Ski rental? More housing? Dammit, Dad. You can't do this. You'll destroy the snowy plover habitat."

RW's mouth opened. Closed. He sat hard on the nearest chair. "Forget what I just said." Like they could. Matt stepped closer. Jeff did, too, but Julia held Henry back.

"What's going on?" Matt asked.

"I can't talk about this. Especially not in front of them," RW said softly. "You have no idea how dangerous this is."

Matt caught Jeff's eye. Jeff shrugged.

Julia stepped forward. "RW, please. Stop your development plans. Nothing is worth the destruction of an entire species. You have thousands of acres. Why put anything on top of a hatchery?"

RW blinked at her as if he was seeing a ghost. "But it's the perfect spot for the school. The kids will love it."

"What?" Matt said.

Jeff studied the plans. "He's right. It's a school. A really cool one, from the looks of it."

Julia cocked her head, looking closely at the plans. "I don't understand. You're building a school in Pueblicito?"

RW smiled for the first time since they'd entered the room. "Did you know the children here have to travel forty minutes on a bus one-way to go to school?"

"Yes," Henry spoke up. "I hate that stupid bus. It doesn't have air-conditioning and the springs are popping out of the seats."

RW motioned for Henry to come forward. "That's unacceptable. And the school you go to—"

"Sucks," Henry finished. "It's like a hundred years old and the teachers are even older."

"Henry," Julia admonished.

"What? It's true."

"I agree with the young man. How can a student learn in these conditions? How can young, bright, teachers be attracted to such a dilapidated school? No, I am building a school in Pueblicito and that is the end of it. I will hire the best teachers and create the best programs in the state and our little friend here will have the best education possible. You can't talk me out of it."

Jeff, Matt and Julia all looked at each other.

"That sounds great, really. I mean, who wouldn't want to go to the school on the beach? I'd do that any day of the week instead of going to math class. But I'd go to math twice a day if we could save the birds. Kids should learn about saving stuff like the environment and creatures who are smaller than us. Can't we do that, too?" Henry asked.

Julia's hand went to her heart. Matt felt a burning pressure behind his eyes. Damn, he was proud of that kid.

"So...*you* want me to move the school off the beach?" RW spoke directly to Henry.

"Yes, sir. And thank you. Sorry, I should have said that first."

RW nodded. "Okay. It's done. Miss Espinoza, perhaps you and I can work together to locate a spot for the school that will not impact your birds."

Julia's eyes were wide with shock. "They're *our* birds, Mr. Harper. And I'd be delighted."

"Excellent," RW said.

Henry fist-pumped the air. "Woot! You aren't as bad as they say."

RW laughed. It was the most casual and easy sound

Matt had ever heard his father make. "Don't tell anyone, son."

When RW winked and messed up Henry's hair and added, "I hope you come back and see me again," it was too much to process. The school, the wink, the hospitality? Matt's head exploded.

What in the hell was happening to his father?

As Jeff, Julia and Henry started to leave the hall, Matt held back.

"We need to talk, Dad," he said.

"Yes, I suppose we do." He seemed old in that moment. Tired. "There's a lot to say, but I've been so screwed up…" RW shook his head, unable to voice the words.

"Me, too, Dad. Later tonight?"

RW nodded and rose to his feet. Before Matt got blindsided again, he took the offensive and threw his arms around RW.

Hugging seemed to be his new thing.

Matt jogged to catch up to Henry and Julia.

"It's like a museum. I can't believe people live here." Henry took in the art, the crystal chandelier and the mosaic tiles while they walked through the long hallway.

"*Living* is such a big word for what goes on in this house. It's nothing like your home. You're really lucky," Matt said.

Henry chewed on that a moment. "Yeah, you're right. It's too quiet here. There's no laughing. No music. No dancing."

"Sometimes there's dancing." Julia's eyes twinkled. "Captain was the greatest of them all. A legend."

He leaned into her, tucked her hair behind her ear and whispered, "There's a lot more where that came from. Better moves than you've ever seen."

She bit her lip. "I'd like to see those moves."

"Later. When you are naked." His whispered words made her shiver in anticipation.

They stepped out into the sunlight. Matt smiled every time he saw Julia's ugly lime-green Cube. When they were young she'd talked of saving enough money to buy her own car. He'd secretly vowed to give her one. Hell, he would've done anything, short of stealing, to make it happen. It must've been quite a day when she drove her very own car off the lot. He wished he'd been there to see it.

Before Julia turned the ignition, she said, "I think I might have misjudged your father."

"You and I both know how he used to be. I have no idea who that man was back there in the hall, but he isn't the RW I grew up on the wrong side of. I say we don't complain and roll with it. Whatever has changed him, it seems like Pueblicito might actually get something good out of the deal."

Julia's cell phone rang inside her purse. She dug around and pulled it out. "*¿Hola?* Okay, we'll be right there." She glanced up at Matt. "Tía Nona asked us to stop by her place on the way home."

"Is everything all right?"

"I don't know, she sounded…strange. Worried. She asked us to come right away."

Julia drove quickly and parked her Cube in Tía Nona's driveway. Just as she was about to knock on the door, they heard Tía Nona inside saying, "Angel left! *¡Dios mio!* She didn't even say goodbye. I can't lose her again."

"We'll find her." It was Tía Alana's voice.

"Just like we did the last time." Tía Flora seemed to agree.

Julia looked at Matt. "Who is this Angel everyone's talking about?"

"I don't know, sweetheart. But your aunts do."

"Angel?" Henry poked his head between them. "She's their sister." Without another word, he opened the door and stepped inside without knocking.

Grabbing Matt's arm, she pulled him back before he stepped over the threshold. "Another sister I didn't know about? One who's in trouble and involved with *your* father? How is that possible?"

Matt took her hand. "Let's go sort it out."

Twenty-Two

Stepping inside Tía Nona's small living room, Julia could feel the nervous energy.

Tía Nona rubbed her red, dripping eyes, which made no sense since she'd always said she was too *malgeniosa* to cry. Tía Flora paced and Tía Alana was… smoking? An open bottle of tequila sat on the floor by the couch.

Julia reached behind her and grabbed Matt's hand. When he took it, her nerves eased to a dull pounding. He had a way of centering her. "What's going on?"

Tía Nona blew her nose and then said, "Angel is gone. I went to her place and it is empty. We have to find her."

"Angel?" Julia asked.

"Yeah, um. Well, you don't know her, she's a…a…"

"Friend," Tía Alana said.

"Cousin," Tía Flora said.

"Neighbor," Tía Nona finished.

Henry snorted. "And they tell me not to lie."

"Henry, why don't you go down the street and visit Anthony? This sounds like adult problems."

"Ah, Mom…"

"Get going."

"Fine."

When Henry left, Matt spoke up. "We know Angel is in trouble. My father hinted that much. Let's start there. We can argue about who she is later."

Nona sighed. "I bet RW is beside himself. He cares for her very deeply. She saved his life, you know."

No, Julia did not know. Out of the corner of her eye, she saw Matt's eyebrows rise, but he didn't say a word.

"What can you tell us about her?" Julia prodded.

Nona sighed. "Not much. We've been sworn to secrecy."

"On account of the gang that is after her." Alana nodded.

"Because she saw too much," Flora finished.

"¡Tontas! Might as well tell them Angel is our baby sister." Nona covered her mouth. "Merida de burro. Forget I said that."

Too late. Tequila had a way of opening Nona's lips.

"Your sister lives here, in Pueblicito, and I've never met her? How is that possible?" Julia asked.

"'Cuz she's been incognito. Like when you wore Nona's wig to RW's party. She's been hiding in plain sight," Flora said.

"The gang must've found her. That's the only reason she'd leave. We need to get to her before they do!" Nona was wailing now.

"Angel thinks she is protecting her family, but we'd be lost without her," Alana said.

"What should we do?" Flora asked.

Matt spoke up. "Let me talk to my father. He has men in place, watching out for Angel. He'll know where she went and what to do next."

Flora pressed her hand to her chest. "See? That man loves Angel. I knew it."

Alana huffed. "He has asked her to marry him half a dozen times. She turns him down on account of the gang."

"And Julia." Flora nodded.

"What about me?" Julia asked.

"Nothing!" Tía Nona gave both her sisters the evil eye. "Go on, Matthew. Call your father. Maybe he can stop her."

Matt stepped outside the house to place the call. It was a strange conversation full of pregnant pauses, cloaks and daggers and deflection, but he got the answers he needed from RW.

Walking back inside, he saw Julia's face light up. She knew even before he said a word that he had good news. That's how connected they were.

Would he ever find that with anyone else?

"Dad says she's fine. He's moved her to a secure location for a while. He says not to worry."

All the women in the room exhaled at once.

"Oh, thank you." Julia rose off the couch and threw her arms around his neck. In front of everyone, she kissed him soundly.

He wrapped his arms around her waist and held her. He didn't want to let go.

"*Madre de Dios*, they are so cute. When's the wedding?" Flora asked with a smile.

Matt looked down and saw that panic had replaced the blood in Julia's face. Her eyes had a wild frenzy to them, too. He was holding a caged animal.

He let her go.

"Let's not get ahead of ourselves," Matt said to the aunts.

Julia took a large step away from him. "Matt's right. Sometimes…" Her cheeks were pale and her brow was furrowed. Her eyes welled. It was her determined face mixed with great sadness. "Sometimes people leave because that's what they're supposed to do. Matt and I won't be getting married. He's leaving tomorrow. His life is not here. I need to… I have to…" She opened the front door. "Walk."

He knew she hadn't been saying goodbye, not really. But the emotions that had been hanging on a precipice this entire weekend slipped when she shut the door. It was like getting crushed by an avalanche.

There really was no future for them.

"Matthew?" Nona's voice broke through the landslide in his head.

He didn't move. Couldn't think.

"Listen to me now, it's important."

He turned toward her voice.

"Remember I had something to show you? Come with me." Nona took his hand and pulled him toward her room. She gently guided him to an old chair and pushed him into it.

"Now, you hear me, Matthew Harper. No two people were ever meant to be together more than you and my Julia."

"She loves someone else." Damn, the words tore through his innards even worse when said out loud.

"That's straight caca from the bull. Julia wants you more than anything, silly boy. She always has. She's just scared. When you left, she went to the bad place. It was all we could do to snatch her from the devil's hands. She's afraid of giving her heart to you again because, if you break it, we might not be able to beat the devil a second time. Do you understand?"

He blinked. "I'd never hurt her. Why would she think that?"

"You tell me. These are the letters she wrote to you when you left. They were all returned unopened." She dropped a large pile of envelopes wrapped in a red ribbon. "Hundreds of them."

He was shocked. "I never got these. I wrote to her, too. Every day until she forgot about me. Until she married someone else."

"Forget about you? Never." Tía Nona shook her head. "She didn't get any letters, *mijo*. Not one."

"Who did this? Who blocked our letters…?" He ran his hand through his hair, suddenly knowing the answer. There were only two people who had wanted to keep them apart. Only two who had told Julia he'd died. "My parents."

Nona rubbed his shoulder. "I would think so, yes. They control this town, it would be nothing for them to control the mail delivery."

Julia'd thought he'd abandoned her before he died. "That's why she moved on so soon." He hadn't meant to say the words aloud, but they slipped out. And that's why he had moved on, too. He'd focused his entire adult life on starting the airline because he couldn't

Twenty-Three

She didn't walk, she ran all the way to the beach. *Our beach.*

Matt was everywhere—in the tall grass, the white sand, the lapping waves. Tonight, when the stars came out, he'd be there, too. Making promises he couldn't keep and soaring over the moon.

Her heart was completely thrashed, but it was still beating. She was alive and determined to stay out of the dark place because she was Henry's mother. She couldn't fail him.

She could do this. Somehow, she'd survive saying goodbye to Matt Harper again and go about the business of living.

Oh, Lord, it was going to hurt. The internal shredding had already begun and would only get worse.

She took her shoes off and walked across the sand.

No snowy plovers here. The patches of grass were too sparse for them and they preferred the other beach with better cover for their hatchery. She dipped her toes in the cold water and tried to breathe. It was hard, what with the crushing ache in her chest.

"Thought I'd find you here." His deep voice rolled over her like a wave. A wish. A promise she had no business hanging on to.

She was too broken to turn around.

"Julia, please." The quake in his words was her undoing.

She went to him. He opened his arms and she put her head on his chest. She fought tears by deeply breathing in his scent. He always calmed her.

Matt and Julia against the world.

"I learned something today," he said softly. "You never got any of my letters."

She sucked in a breath. "You must not have gotten any of mine, either. The ones I sent before I went to your funeral."

He tipped her chin up. "I didn't. I had no idea all that you went through and I am so, so sorry. Hell, I wouldn't have survived. No way. Just shows how strong you are."

She shook her head. "I'm not strong, Matt."

"Wrong, babe." He kissed her cheek. "I just wanted you to know that I understand now why you needed to go forward without me."

"Part of me never did go forward."

"Same here. You've always been inside me, Julia. A sweet song I never forgot the words to. You are in my bones. In my heart." He kissed the other cheek. "I love you, Julia. Always have. I told you that in those fifty letters."

He still loved her? She covered her mouth and blinked the hot tears, unable to speak.

He went on, "Someone blocked our correspondence. Not certain, but I'd bet it was my mother."

"Your mother?" Her voice cracked.

He rubbed her back. "Yep. My father was having his own issues. I think she was the one trying to keep us apart. She has strange ideas about class. And, honestly, she probably was jealous of us. She didn't know how to love. Seeing us happy probably ticked her off."

Julia held him as he continued. "She wasn't a great mom."

Except…maybe she was. Julia understood the gripping painful decisions that came with motherhood. What would she have done to protect her son from a terrible mistake?

"She was trying to save you, Matt. You were only seventeen with a glorious future ahead. She didn't want you to ruin your life with a mistake. I understand that now." She loved him. Would always, but he deserved to know the truth. She owed him that much, so she took a deep breath and told him, "Henry is your son. He's the best gift you ever gave me."

His hand froze on her shoulder. His eyes widened. His mouth opened. No sound came out. She pressed her hand to his chest to feel the thundering train beneath her palm.

"He's…he's mine?"

"Henry Matthew Harper is most definitely yours. I've never slept with anyone other than you. You're his daddy."

"You named him after me?" He scrubbed his jaw, as if feeling for the beard that wasn't there. "But I thought… He said his father was a pilot who died in Afghanistan…oh. It was me this whole time?"

"Yes."

"Henry said the only guy you ever loved was…" He blinked. "Me, again?"

"Yes."

Slowly his face cracked open like a sunrise. "I'm the only man you've ever slept with?"

She narrowed her eyes. "After everything I said, that's the one thing you're honing in on?"

He swooped her up in his arms. "No way, sweetheart. What I heard was I'm a daddy to the greatest kid on the planet and the one true love to the best woman in the universe. What I'm honing in on is ten years I missed making love to my woman. If we don't start now, we'll never catch up."

He laid her down on the sand and kissed her as if he'd never stop.

Her heart was racing. He tasted so good that she let her mind center on him and not on all the revelations that had come tonight. He nibbled down her jawline and kissed her neck. She laughed beneath him. He cupped her breast through her blouse and rolled her nipple under the material.

"Matt, the sun hasn't gone down yet."

"And?" He pressed his erection against her. Being the pirate's harlot that she was, her hips lifted in response.

"Um, people can see us?"

"Is that a question?" He smiled and bent to suck her nipple through her blouse.

"Oh. You are so bad."

"I'll show you bad. Take your shirt off."

"If someone walks by, they will see us."

He ran his hand up the inside of her shorts until he found her panties. "I want these off, too."

"Matt."

"Julia. I am going to make love to you right now. On our beach. The same sand where I once asked you to marry me and you said yes. The same spot where we promised each other forever. I don't break my promises, babe."

Her mind was spinning.

He pulled off her shorts, panties included. "Do you want me to make you come three times right now?" He petted her and she was already losing her mind.

"Only three?"

"Babe, you are killing me here. I might not be able to wait for you to make up your mind."

She rubbed his erection through his jeans. "I want you as deep as you can get. Hurry."

He unzipped his pants. He lifted her hips with his hands and eased himself inside. He felt so good. The feelings and words rolled over her.

Home. Mine. Matt.

And when he pounded into her, she rolled with him, giving as good as she got. She cried out, forgetting she was on public land and could get arrested for indecency if the sheriff decided to drive by today.

He kissed her, swallowing her sounds. He lifted her hips again. In. Out. Hard. Fast. It was difficult to catch her breath. They were both glistening with sweat and sand stuck to her bottom. And still he kept on electrifying every sweet spot inside her.

She cried out again, whimpered really, because the feelings were so strong. She gripped his butt and he shuddered. A few more thrusts and, heaven help her, she came again. Three. How did he do that?

He rolled to the side to look at her. She quickly pulled up her shorts and straightened her blouse.

He laughed and zipped up his jeans. Then he kissed her on the tip of her nose. "I love you, Julia. I always have."

She sighed. "I love you, my sweet bad boy. It's going to kill me when you leave. But I understand, Matt. I really do. You have a life waiting for you away from here. An airline to run. Your dreams are right there, ready to be grabbed."

He rubbed her chin. "Julia. I am not leaving you or my son. I love you both. Come with me."

He loves our son. It made her want to cry with happiness and grief. "We can't. Henry has school and his family here. His friends. If we go, we won't know anyone. You'll be flying all over the world and we'll be alone in a strange place. That wouldn't be good for a kid like Henry. And what about my education? And taking the bar. I can't do that in Asia."

He kneaded his neck. "Must be some way to make this work."

All the wonder of earlier faded and she started to cry. She'd found love and yet still she couldn't have him?

"How?" she asked. "If you stay here, you'll have to live near RW. You hate Plunder Cove because of him. I can't ask you to be anywhere near that man's thumb. But even worse, you'll give up your dream of owning your own airline. I can't take that from you."

He didn't say a word but she saw the pain in his eyes.

"I saw you up there. Flying is your passion. Your life. I want you to be happy. You deserve this, Matt."

"Henry?"

"We don't tell him. His father died before he was born. He's used to that. Why confuse the situation?"

"No! I won't be an absent father. I want…"

"Everything. I know. But as a parent, you do what's best for your child. That's why I won't beg you to stay, no matter how much I *need*…" Her voice cracked. She shook her head. "This isn't up to me. It's about doing what's right for Henry. And for you."

He stood. "No, dammit! I don't get any say in this?"

She grabbed his hand and kissed his palm. "I won't be the one to crush your life. Please, Matt, decide what's best for you—Asia or Plunder Cove." She rose, too, and stood on her toes to kiss his jaw. "I love you, Matt. So much that I'll let you go."

Twenty-Four

Matt was walking in the street when Alfred pulled up beside him. "Need a ride?"

For the first time in his life, he felt like walking. Hell, maybe he'd hoof it right off the ends of the earth. He was replaying the beach scene in his head.

He'd had the woman he loved in his arms. He'd given her his heart. He had a son! Julia'd said she loved him.

So how could she even suggest he fly away alone?

The worst part? She was right.

Dammit, he *wanted* to go to Asia to fly his own planes. It was the one thing that had saved him in Afghanistan when he'd thought Julia had married another guy. He *wanted* to live somewhere where his father wasn't.

But that was before he'd seen Julia two days ago.

Before he'd known the truth about what had happened between them ten years ago.

He wanted her back in his life. No, *want* was too soft a word for how much he desired Julia.

She loved him.

Add Henry to the equation and Matt was the luckiest man on earth. He shook his head, reality smacking him upside his brain again.

Sweet God. I have a family!

And a crazy extended family to boot.

How could he walk away from all of that?

If he could take them all to Asia, where he could fly and run his airline, everything would be perfect. For him. Not so much for all the people he loved.

And who said he couldn't run an airline from California? He could have it all, and give it all to Julia and Henry, too.

He wouldn't be a selfish prick like his own father had been. RW had always put Harper Industries first, before everything and everyone. Matt had never felt like he or his siblings were important or wanted.

He would do things differently.

But before he could do that, before he could stay in Plunder Cove, he had to settle things with his father once and for all.

"So was that a no on the ride?" Alfred interrupted his thoughts.

Matt shook his head. "I'll drive."

"Dad, are you in there?" He knocked on his father's study door.

RW opened up. "Matthew, come in. Would you like a drink? You look a bit frazzled."

Frazzled? He'd been through the ringer. "I could use a beer."

"Sit." RW motioned toward his leather couch and handed Matt a beer from the minifridge. "What's on your mind, son?"

Son. He took a sip before asking the burning question. "Dad, did you know that Henry is my son?"

RW sat next to him. "He's handsome and smart. He has your eyes. Of course he's a Harper."

"Is that why you're building the new school?"

"Can't have my grandson traveling eighty-plus minutes a day on the bus. And the education at that school stinks. Henry and his buddies deserve better."

Matt shook his head. "How long have you known?"

"Not long. Angel clued me in to the possibility, so I did a little investigating myself."

Angel. Again. "Where is she, Dad?"

"She's safe. Staying out of the limelight for a while until things die down."

"Tell her that her sisters are really worried about her."

"I will, son. She's going to be okay. There's nothing I won't do to protect her."

Matt leaned back on the couch and crossed his arms behind his head. "I feel the same about Julia, but she wants me to leave Plunder Cove. Go my own way and ignore the fact that I have a son and family here."

"That doesn't sound like her. What did you do?"

"Me? Why would you assume I'm in the wrong?"

RW let out a deep breath. "Sorry. That's not what I meant. Tell me why she is giving you the boot."

Sorry? That was the first apology Matt had ever heard his father make.

"She's not giving me the…well, I mean, sort of. She says it's up to me to decide to stay or go. She knows how much I want to fly my own planes but she and Henry don't want to go to Asia. That's not a life that would work for them. But she's worried that if I don't go I will eventually hate her for setting limits on my life."

"She's a smart lady." RW templed his hands in front of his nose. "There's another option. You've probably considered it, but I'll lay it out anyway. You could stay here and operate an airline for Harper Industries, flying in clients as we discussed. Grow that part of our business to something bigger even. You'd have free rein to fly whenever, wherever you want. Maybe even partner with the Forest Service to provide search-and-rescue support like I heard you love to do. And we'd have the best planes money could buy because you'd pick out each one for the fleet. How's that sound?"

Like his father was trying to buy him. Matt threw up his hands. "Why do you want to keep me here, Dad? I don't get it."

RW swallowed hard. "Because I was a horrible father. You deserved better. I want to give you something better now, while I still can."

For the fifty-billionth time this weekend, Matt was floored. "I don't know what to say."

RW lifted one shoulder. "What's to say? I'm sorry, Matthew. From the toxic relationship with your mother to the way I blamed you for my faults to forcing you to leave Julia, I made your life hell.

"I was caught up in trying to grow my father's company and keep the competitors at bay while fighting with your mother. There was no safe place for me. No peace. What I didn't know was that I was also sick and that sickness nearly broke me. I was out of my mind with debilitating paranoia when I sent you, Jeffrey and Chloe away. I was afraid for your safety. It was the last good act I did as a father. I can't expect you to forgive me, but I hope you will one day let me be a part of your life again.

"I want to try to be what you need. If not for you, then for your son."

RW took a sip of water. His hands shook.

Matt was stunned by the apology and realized it was his turn. "Well, looking back, I have to admit that it wasn't all you. I had sort of a wild streak."

"Sort of?" RW laughed.

"Okay, a wide wild streak. My behavior and your illness weren't a good mix, I guess. I'm sorry for my part in all that happened."

"I'm being treated now, son. Don't worry. It was difficult back then to handle a teen who liked to push my buttons."

Matt grinned. "Don't all teenagers like to push buttons? Ordering me not to see Julia, though…that was a big mistake. Sure, I was only seventeen, but I loved her like crazy. I still do. Your threat has haunted me for ten years. What you did changed both of our lives. You aren't still planning to release the secrets that could hurt her family, are you?"

"They're not my secrets. One day, the truth will come out, but only when Angel is ready. And when she is, I'll be by her side, or perhaps, in front of her, to shield her from harm."

"She sounds like an amazing woman. I hope I get to meet her one day."

"That's up to her. I'm letting her call the shots right now because she's in a predicament and she's also the reason we're all here, back in Plunder Cove together. She pushed me to be a better man. Helped me get treatment. Taught me how to hope. Do you know which questions keep me up at night?"

"What are the stock prices?"

RW shook his head. "Will an undeserving man like me finally be allowed to get a happily-ever-after? Can a horrible father fix the past? Is one person strong enough to pay back hundreds of years of abuse? These are the things I struggle to grasp—redemption and love. I don't deserve either one, but I'm still reaching, still asking."

Matt studied his father and realized he'd never known him at all. But this guy pouring out his heart? Matt might like getting to know *him*.

"Want a little piece of advice from a man who has been in the trenches?" RW asked.

"Sure."

"A woman who sees you for who you are and loves you anyway doesn't come around often. Especially one who is willing to forgo her own happiness so you can have a shot at yours." RW leaned forward and put his hand on Matt's knee. "Find your angel and hang on with both hands. Then pray to God you don't screw it up."

Matt nodded. "Thanks, Dad."

"Hell, son. Why are you still sitting here gabbing with your old man? Go!"

Julia recognized Matt's rap on her door. With her heart in her throat, she opened it, surprised to see him on one knee on her doorstep with a yellow chick cupped in his hands.

"What on earth?"

Matt began, "Julia Espinoza, will you—?"

The neighbor's door opened and Tía Nona peeked her head out. "I'm watching the baby over here. What're you doing on the porch, Matthew?"

"He's fine, *tía*. Go back inside," Julia said.

But when did Tía Nona ever do as she was told?

Matt tried again. "Julia Espinoza—"

"Maria. That's her middle name. Might want to add that in there," Tía Nona said.

He let out a soft breath. "Okay. Julia Maria Espinoza, will—"

"Can't forget her mother's maiden name. It wouldn't be proper," Tía Alana yelled out her window. "It's Martinez."

"Where's the ring?" Tía Flora shouted from her window.

Matt lifted the yellow chick higher. "I didn't have time for a ring, so I snagged this little guy from the Casa Larga kitchen gardens. I hope he'll buy me some brownie points. I know how much you love birds and figure the jewelry can come later."

Henry popped his head out the door. "Hey, Matt. What are you doing on the ground with a chick? Did you fall or something? Need help getting up?" Henry reached to help lift him and all the aunts yelled, "No!"

Tía Nona hissed, "Let the man speak."

Matt looked around and noticed half the town was staring at him. He barely flinched. He turned back to Julia and kept his focus solely on her. "You are so damned beautiful. So out of my league. Sweet and spicy. Strong and gentle. The day I popped wheelies in front of Juanita's, I knew you were mine. My love, my home. I don't want to live anywhere without you."

Tears were flowing down her cheeks. "What about your airline? You can't pass up this opportunity!"

"*You* are my opportunity. My one chance at happiness. My family." He looked into her eyes and then at Henry. "I have everything I want right here in Pueblicito. *Our* town. And I'm staying." He took a deep breath. "Julia Maria Martinez Espinoza, will you marry—"

"Yes! Oh, God, yes." She pulled him to his feet and gently handed the chick to Henry. Then she took her opportunity and kissed the daylights out of him.

The entire town erupted in cheers.

Epilogue

Chloe went above and beyond to plan the best wedding a pirate could ever have.

The ceremony was to take place in the gazebo where Matt and Julia first kissed. She'd decorated the wood structure with white twinkling lights and fragrant flowers. The walkway to the gazebo was draped with a long pink sash and covered in memories. She'd blown up the pictures from Matt's camera and collected several others from people all over town. Even Alfred contributed to the walkway of photos. The best pictures, hands down, were the ones with Henry, Matt and Julia together. Love and happiness jumped out of each shot.

Inside the house, Julia waited with Maria and Linda. Julia was doing her best not to pass out.

"*¡Guau!* That dress is gorgeous. Can I wear it after you?" Maria asked.

Julia hiked her eyebrow. "Something you're not telling us?"

"Nah. Thinking ahead in case Jaime finds his balls."

Her cousins hugged her carefully.

"Can I get in there, too?" a voice said behind her.

"Juanita!" Julia opened her arms farther to let Juanita into the hugging pile. When they all released one another, Julia said, "I heard you closed the café for my wedding. Glad you made it."

"I came to wish you love and happiness, but I can't stay. Something has come up and I have to leave Plunder Cove." Juanita's voice sounded strained.

"Something serious?"

Juanita waved her hand like it was nothing, but Julia saw the tremble in her slender fingers.

"Tell me. Maybe I can help. I'm going to be a lawyer, you know." Julia smiled. Juanita was the one who'd encouraged her to go to college. She was also the one who'd found a donor to help pay some of the educational bills.

"Yes. You are." Juanita cupped Julia's cheek. "I'm so proud of you. Look at all you have accomplished! Saving the birds, moving the school. You did that. You. No one else. Never forget how special you are, *nene*."

Julia blinked. *Nene*. The translation for the word could be darling, little one, or my baby. Tía Nona called her that all the time. No one else did.

"I won't forget. No matter what happens," Juanita said.

Julia frowned. It sounded like a forever goodbye. Julia pulled Juanita into her arms and held on tight.

"Stay safe, Angel," she whispered. "Please come

back when you can. Or let your family help you. We are stronger in numbers and we all love you."

Juanita—Angel—bristled in Julia's arms, startled. And a second later she relaxed, still holding on tight. "How'd you know?"

"You were so kind and gentle to me. You gave me and Matt a safe place to be ourselves. A haven of safety and warmth. When I was sad, you listened. Happy, you laughed. Sick at heart, you nursed my wounds. You fed me, gave me shelter and loving acceptance. I can't tell you how many times I wished you were my mother."

Angel pulled back. Tears streamed down her face. "In my heart I was. I wish I could've been your mother in all other ways, as well."

Julia's eyes went wide as she realized the truth. Then she cried, too. "Trust me, Mama. You were."

Matt stood next to the gazebo on the grassy hill, overlooking the ocean. He patiently waited for Julia— his lover, his heart. Beside him, RW and Jeff kept him company. He grinned. Harper men always looked good in tuxedos. Henry, the ring man, walked down the aisle as Chloe had taught him. Only, at the end, he ran up and gave Matt a fist bump. It wasn't scripted, but it was perfect.

RW looked over Matt's shoulder toward the beach. He seemed preoccupied.

"What's up?" Matt asked.

RW frowned. "See that skiff? Where'd it come from?"

"Call it in."

RW pulled his cell phone out. "Talk to me about the skiff…Who? Are you sure?…Okay. Keep an eye on it."

Matt leaned over. "And?"

"Cristina, a friend of Angel's. She came to the wedding."

"Do you know this friend?"

RW's gaze scanned the crowd. "Yes. She was an informant, giving us intel on the gang that's been after Angel. Angel's been trying to get Cristina to come here for her own protection."

"That's good, right?"

"Yeah, except I don't see Angel. She wanted to be here."

Matt scanned the crowd. Everyone he'd ever known smiled back at him—including the Forestry Service guys who'd welcomed him as part of their team.

Working with Harper Industries, and with search and rescue, he was going to be flying a lot. And the best part was, he could sleep in his own bed and wake up tangled in Julia's arms. Maybe Henry would climb in sometimes, too.

Hell, Matt couldn't wait to start his new life right here in Plunder Cove.

The cell buzzed in RW's pocket. RW glanced at the text and looked out to the shore.

Matt followed his gaze. "Dad. The skiff is gone."

RW gave him a short nod. "Later. We'll find her."

Jeff leaned over. "You two done yakking? The bridesmaids are lined up."

The music started and Linda walked down the aisle followed by Maria. Linda winked at him and Maria raised her fist. Welcome to the crazy family.

Guess what, ladies, you are now part of mine.

The "Wedding March" started and the most beautiful woman in the world smiled at him.

My Julia. My home.

He nearly fell to his knees with gratitude. He had his planes, his motorcycle and more toys than any man could want, but none of it mattered without people to love. Now he had a son, a brother, a sister, a father he was trying to get to know, an extended family and his own angel. It was more bounty than he ever knew existed.

What more could a pirate want?

* * * * *

Will RW find Angel?
Will Jeff come home to find his dreams, too?

Find out in the next Plunder Cove novel
from Kimberley Troutte,
available February 2019!

COMING NEXT MONTH FROM

Available September 4, 2018

#2611 KEEPING SECRETS
Billionaires and Babies • by Fiona Brand
Billionaire Damon Smith's sexy assistant shared his bed and then vanished for a year. Now she's returned—with his infant daughter! Can he work through the dark secrets Zara's still hiding and claim the family he never knew he wanted?

#2612 RUNAWAY TEMPTATION
Texas Cattleman's Club: Bachelor Auction
by Maureen Child
When Caleb attends a colleague's wedding, the last person he expects to leave with is the runaway bride! He offers Shelby a temporary hideout on his ranch. But soon the sizzle between them has this wealthy cowboy wondering if seduction will convince her to stay...

#2613 STRANGER IN HIS BED
The Masters of Texas • by Lauren Canan
Brooding Texan Wade Masters brings his estranged wife home from the hospital with amnesia. This new, sensual, *kind* Victoria makes him feel things he never has before. But when he discovers the explosive truth, will their second chance at love be as doomed as their first?

#2614 ONE NIGHT SCANDAL
The McNeill Magnates • by Joanne Rock
Actress Hannah must expose the man who hurt her sister. Sexy rancher Brock has clues, but amnesia means he can't remember them—or his one night with her! Still, he pursues her with a focus she can't resist. What happens when he finds out everything?

#2615 THE RELUCTANT HEIR
The Jameson Heirs • by HelenKay Dimon
Old-money heir Carter Jameson has a family who thrives on deceit. He's changing that by finding the woman who knows devastating secrets about his father. The problem? He wants her, maybe more than he wants redemption. And what he thinks she knows is nothing compared to the truth...

#2616 PLAYING MR. RIGHT
Switching Places • by Kat Cantrell
CEO Xavier LeBlanc must resist his new employee—his inheritance is on the line! But there's more to her than meets the eye...because she's working undercover to expose fraud at his charity. Too bad Xavier is falling faster than her secrets are coming to light...

YOU CAN FIND MORE INFORMATION ON UPCOMING HARLEQUIN® TITLES, FREE EXCERPTS AND MORE AT WWW.HARLEQUIN.COM.

HDCNM0818

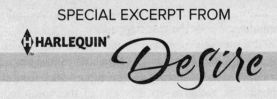
Shelby Arthur stared at her own reflection and hardly
recognized herself. She supposed all brides felt like
that on their wedding day, but for her, the effect was
terrifying.

She was looking at a stranger wearing an old-fashioned
gown with long, lacy sleeves, a cinched waist and full
skirt, and a neckline that was so high she felt as if she
were choking. Shelby was about to get married in a dress
she hated, a veil she didn't want, to a man she wasn't sure
she liked, much less loved. How did she get to this point?

"Oh, God. What am I doing?"

She'd left her home in Chicago to marry Jared
Goodman. But now that he was home in Texas, under
his awful father's thumb, Jared was someone she didn't

even know. Her whirlwind romance had morphed into a nightmare and now she was trapped.

Shelby met her own eyes in the mirror and read the desperation there. In a burst of fury, she ripped her veil off her face. Then, blowing a stray auburn lock from her forehead, she gathered up the skirt of the voluminous gown in both arms and hurried down the hall and toward the nearest exit.

And ran smack into a brick wall.

Well, that was what it felt like.

A tall, gorgeous brick wall who grabbed her upper arms to steady her, then smiled down at her with humor in his eyes. He had enough sex appeal to light up the city of Houston, and the heat from his hands, sliding down her body, made everything inside her jolt into life.

"Aren't you headed the wrong way?" he asked, and the soft drawl in his deep voice awakened a single thought in her mind.

Oh, boy.

Don't miss
Runaway Temptation
by USA TODAY *bestselling author Maureen Child,
the first in the Texas Cattleman's Club:
Bachelor Auction series.*

*Available September 2018 wherever
Harlequin® Desire books and ebooks are sold.*

www.Harlequin.com

LOVE
Harlequin
romance?

Join our Harlequin community to share your thoughts and connect with other romance readers!

Be the first to find out about promotions, news, and exclusive content!

Sign up for the Harlequin e-newsletter and download a free book from any series at

www.TryHarlequin.com

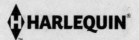

THE WORLD IS BETTER WITH

Romance

Harlequin has everything from contemporary, passionate and heartwarming to suspenseful and inspirational stories.

Whatever your mood, we have a romance just for you!

Connect with us to find your next great read, special offers and more.

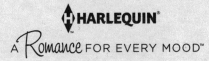